Daisy Chain Dream

D0550362

Also in this trilogy:

1. Daisy Chain War
2. Bread and Sugar

Joan O'Neill

Daisy Chain Dream

**Hodder
Children's
Books**

a division of Hodder Headline Limited

In memory of my mother, Josephine Manahan, who gave me the inspiration, and my father, William Patrick Manahan, who passed on the talent.

Text copyright © 1994 Joan O'Neill

First published in paperback in Ireland in 1994
by Poolbeg, a division of Poolbeg Enterprises Ltd

This paperback edition published in Great Britain in 2003
by Hodder Children's Books

The right of Joan O'Neill to be identified as the Author of
the Work has been asserted by her in accordance with
the Copyright, Designs and Patents Act 1988.

10 9 8 7 6 5 4 3

A Catalogue record for this book is available from
the British Library

ISBN 0 340 85468 5

Typeset in Bembo by Avon DataSet Ltd,
Bidford-on-Avon, Warwickshire

Printed and bound in Great Britain by
Clays Ltd, St Ives plc

The paper and board used in this paperback by Hodder Children's Books are natural recyclable products made from wood grown in sustainable forests. The manufacturing processes conform to the environmental regulations of the country of origin.

Hodder Children's Books
A Division of Hodder Headline Limited
338 Euston Road
London NW1 3BH

When you are old and grey and full of sleep,
And nodding by the fire, take down this book,
And slowly read, and dream of the soft look
Your eyes had once, and of their shadows deep;

How many loved your moments of glad grace,
And loved your beauty with love false or true,
But one man loved the pilgrim soul in you,
And loved the sorrows of your changing face;

And bending down beside the glowing bars,
Murmur, a little sadly, how Love fled
And paced upon the mountains overhead
And hid his face amid a crowd of stars.

William Butler Yeats, 'When You are Old'

Acknowledgements

With special thanks to my editor, Emily Thomas, for her enthusiasm and initiative. Thanks too Honor Wilson-Fletcher, Nancy Cooper, Venetia Gosling, and all at Hodder (Children's) for their support. Thanks to the Art Department at Hodder for the inspirational covers. Thanks to Carolyn Caughey for suggesting them.

Particular thanks to Jonathan Lloyd of Curtis Brown for his meticulous care of all my work.

As ever my thanks to my beloved daughters, Elizabeth and Laura, for their inspiration from the beginning.

1

Mrs Keogh was cooking the breakfast. Her skin was dull, and beads of perspiration glistened on her upper lip. Yet curiosity made her eyes sparkle, and mobilised her face into expressions of girlish enthusiasm. Her hair was concealed by a turban, and she wore a wrap-over apron to protect her dress from the spurts of fat that were hissing from the sausages sizzling in the frying pan.

'Oh it's true they're the talk of the nation, La la la lala la la la.'

Without removing the cigarette that was dangling from her lips, she greeted Gertie as she entered the kitchen.

'Top of the morning to you.'

'How many times have I told you not to smoke while you're cooking?' Gertie reached out and removed Mrs Keogh's cigarette.

'Ouch.' Mrs Keogh grimaced and, licking her lips, began sliding the sausages on to a large plate, warm from the oven.

'Is it too early to start on the rashers?'

Gertie glanced at the clock. 'They should all be down soon, though I wouldn't bank on it.'

'Have a bit more confidence,' Mrs Keogh began peeling rashers from their greaseproof paper on to the pan, 'else you'll never make a go of it. I'll do the eggs while they're having their porridge.'

'It's a wonder they don't burst with all the food you pile on their plates.'

'That's what they're here for. Most of them haven't seen a bit of meat since before the war. If we give them value for money, they'll be back.'

The smell of bacon permeated the dining-room, and filtered up through the house. Mrs Keogh's loud rendition of 'If I knew you were coming, I'd have baked a cake' greeted the first of the morning's sleepy guests.

Gertie cut home-made brown bread into thick slices, and made butter twirls out of the country butter from the Monument Creamery. It had been three months since the Doyles had decided to turn their home, Santa Maria, Victoria Terrace, Dun Laoghaire, into a guest-house for holidaymakers. April was a beautiful month, ideal for putting the house in order. The wind blew in from the sea, cool and fresh, and snapped at the clothes-line. The curtains billowed, and Mrs Keogh polished every surface until the house was gleaming. Even the Waterford glass had been washed and returned to its cabinet, where it winked and sparkled in the sunshine. Rugs were beaten, drains gushed with water, doors were slammed, and windows that had not been opened for years were cranked up and down.

Gertie was busy again, and happy.

Mrs Keogh sang as she handled every object in the house, and put new lavender bags in linen drawers. Gertie took her canteen of cutlery out of its box, and her silver tea service from the cabinet, wedding presents that had never been used, and put them on the serving table in the dining-room. Boxes of delph and china, put away for Karen and Lizzie, were carefully lifted down from the attic. The house was cleaner than it had ever been.

It angered Bill, Gertie's husband, when something he was searching for had either disappeared or was in a new place. Any change disturbed him, and Gertie's new energy and happiness seemed to him to be an affectation. As she worked with Mrs Keogh, he watched anxiously. When Mrs Keogh would say, 'Do you need this or will I throw that out?' his answer was always the same. 'Leave it.' When Mrs Keogh asked him why he was so irritable, he said, 'She'll make herself sick with all this running up and down stairs and cleaning.'

'Relax,' Mrs Keogh said. 'It's only a phase. She'll calm down as soon as the guests arrive and she's into her routine.'

Bill was not so sure. He bought Gertie a new washing-machine that clamoured in the kitchen as it washed the clothes, while jars and earthenware crocks clanked together as Gertie filled them with home-made marmalade. The idea of turning their home into a guest-house had come from Mrs Keogh, when Gertie and she had been talking about the emptiness of the house since Gran's death. Bill objected, but Gertie's enthusiasm won the day.

'It's one way to make money, and with Lizzie getting married in New York we could use it. And there's Karen and Paul to think of.'

'The Lord will provide,' Bill retorted. 'Anyway, there's no privacy when you open your house to strangers.'

'It's only for the summer. Three months – if that. And we'll have the place to ourselves for the winter.'

Bill frowned and bashed his newspaper.

Gertie said, 'It's either that or sell it. What do we need all those bedrooms for with the family gone?'

The days had loomed long and heavy for Gertie after Gran's death. Lizzie, her daughter, had left her job as a nurse in England, and had gone to work in New York to be near her fiancé, Pete Scanlon. Lizzie had dreamt about her wedding day for as long as Gertie could remember: walking slowly down the aisle in a long white dress, swirling skirt, long train, Pete by her side, teasing her to hide his shyness, the photographers on the lawn. Vicky, her bridesmaid, dressed in coral blue, Gran scattering rose petals from her little cloth bag.

Gertie thought of all the times she had objected to Lizzie's marriage. 'You're too young to fly the nest,' she would say to her. 'Only finished your exams. What's the rush?'

The truth was that Gertie did not want Lizzie to leave home. 'What'll we do without all this?' she would say, surveying the chaotic bedroom, clothes scattered everywhere, drawers pulled out.

In spite of everything Gertie said, Lizzie left home,

and her bedroom had been empty until now. At least if the season was good, Gertie and Bill would be able to afford the trip to America, some new clothes for the occasion, and perhaps a little financial assistance with the cost of the reception.

Gertie's spirits lifted as it began to dawn on her how much she was looking forward to seeing Lizzie again. Karen, her eldest daughter, had moved into the basement with her husband Paul, but Gertie was determined not to intrude. Solitude was precious when the children were small and Gran was alive. She had craved it because it was a rare time of peacefulness, when she could gather her spirits together and recover from the everyday hurly-burly. Now her solitude was filled with anxiety, relieved only by visits from John, Karen's son. Visits that she cherished. The weather had affected her too.

The winter had gone on too long and Gertie told herself that at fifty-five years of age, she was not ready to cross the bridge into old age. Doctor Gregory, the new English doctor, said she was suffering from depression. Gertie herself felt that if she had a purpose, her life would settle, and she would free herself from the burden of her solitude.

Gertie and Bill moved their personal belongings into the breakfast room at the back of the kitchen, including the bed they had shared since their marriage, almost thirty-four years before.

Rationing during the war had left the British people

ravenous, and they were coming to Ireland in droves during the summer months, in search of good food. Industry in Britain had come alive again, and the war damage was being repaired. For the first time since the war, the British had money in their pockets, and they wanted to refresh their palates with the flavour of home-cured bacon, Irish butter and beef. Guest-houses sprang up overnight in Dun Laoghaire. As Mr Mulvey, the manager of McCullough's drapery shop, said, 'Where there's space, there's a bed.'

Mrs Keogh had taken on the job of cook without a quibble. It tickled Gertie to wonder what Gran would think if she could see her greeting 'them foreigners, with strange accents' and being friendly to them. She could imagine Gran saying, 'We burnt them out in the twenties, and now you're welcoming them with open arms.'

Gertie had no retroactive guilt. She was sure that she was just in her dealings: feeding the guests well and giving value for money. They also had the choice of coming down to breakfast in the dining-room, or having their breakfast served in bed.

Turning towards the dining-room, she gave a welcoming smile to the woman sitting at one of the check-clothed tables.

'Good morning, Mrs Turnbull. Did you sleep well?'

'Like a log.'

Mrs Turnbull's husband joined her, explaining his lateness. She did not want to share any part of the last dreary half-hour of her husband's litany. Her attention was focused on Gertie.

'We went on the coach to Wicklow yesterday,' she said. 'What beautiful countryside. I think there'll be a lot of visitors here soon.' She cast her eyes towards the window. 'In spite of the rain.'

'I hope so,' Gertie said. 'It's early days still.'

She was thinking of the money Gran had left her; she had spent it redecorating the ten bedrooms in pastel shades of pinks, greens, blues and yellows, so that each room was distinguished by its colour. Her shopping sprees took her along the Dublin quays, among the antique shops, to buy washstands, floral basins and matching jugs, wardrobes, chests of drawers, an assortment of tables for the dining-room, linen tablecloths.

Each table was decorated with sprigs of flowers in tiny bowls. New beds had been delivered, and the sewing-machine whirred for hours on end as Karen made curtains. Then there were the wages to pay; thirty shillings a week to Mrs Keogh, and fifteen to Biddy Plunkett whom Gertie employed as a waitress. Gertie liked Biddy and knew that her experience as a waitress in the Roman Café would come in useful when she was serving the tables. Biddy had started her new job at the beginning of June.

'Is there no one else available?' Mrs Keogh had asked disapprovingly when she opened the hall door to Biddy that first morning. Mrs Keogh was in her late fifties and Gertie suspected that she was jealous of Biddy.

'She won't stay,' she had said, hinting at Biddy's instability and her own reliability. As the days went by, she bossed Biddy, and listed her shortcomings with such regularity that one day Biddy had lost her temper and flung down the pile of washing she was carrying in from the clothes-line.

'Have you looked in the mirror lately, Mrs Keogh?' she had shouted.

'Why?'

'Because whoever knit your face dropped a stitch.'

'How dare you!'

A few days later when Gertie asked Mrs Keogh to stay and serve the evening meals, she refused. She wanted to be home to get her husband's dinner, which, she said, had to be on the table at six o'clock sharp.

Biddy had offered her services, glad of the extra money.

Fat spattered as Mrs Keogh arranged plates of rashers, sausages, eggs, black and white pudding, and tomatoes, and handed them to Gertie. The dining-room filled up as the guests came straggling down, nodding to one another.

'Eeeeeh. Lovely morning.'

'Och yes. We're off to Killarney today.'

Scottish, Yorkshire and Lancashire accents mingled, and drifted around the dining-room as the guests finished their meals, and Biddy cleared the tables.

Biddy did not mind the work because she nurtured secret ambitions of her own. She longed to be a fashion designer and wear her own elaborate creations. A career like that would provide her with a place in life, where she might own a car someday, and drive around in grand style. She was good at sketching. Everybody said so. Already she was beginning to set herself apart from her sisters and friends, the work giving her a good excuse to do so.

'What's the matter with you, Biddy?' Mrs Keogh asked. 'You're not listening to a word I'm saying.'

'Sorry, Mrs Keogh. I was thinking.'

'Not to be recommended at this hour of the morning. We're too busy. Now get that dining-room cleared.'

Biddy was dressed scantily. Her darned dress was partly concealed by her frilly new apron. In her eyes there was a tentative expression, and her dark hair, held back with a white-peaked band, offset her complexion. Gertie had bought her uniform, and when Mrs Keogh insisted on a dress-rehearsal, she declared that Gertie was suffering from delusions of grandeur.

Biddy was young and enthusiastic; she unnerved people because her ambition made her different. In a seaside town like Dun Laoghaire everyone was recognisable, either from their background or their place of work. Biddy was not. She refused to be servile or cringing. Instead, she was proud and workmanlike, and popular with the guests.

Mrs Keogh glanced at the clock. 'You haven't started on the rooms yet.'

The blow of her reproach fell on deaf ears.

'The day isn't long enough,' Biddy complained, knowing that her work had fallen behind because she had been listening to one of the guests, eager for conversation, telling her terrible life story. She also liked to hear talk of places she had never been, places she recognised from her Geography schoolbook. Places like Leeds and Bradford, where the woollen mills were. One family had come all the way from Spain with their seven-year-old daughter, Carmelita. Carmelita had dusky skin, and her black hair was braided and coiled around her head. Gold earrings glinted in her ears, and she had ribbons to match all the exotic colours of her dresses.

'Buenos días, Biddy,' she would call, and everyone would laugh delightedly at her accent.

Biddy would smile patiently at the guests, her interest encouraging more conversation. Inexpert and young as she was, she managed to make Mrs Keogh feel foolish. Mrs Keogh's resentment of Biddy affected her posture and the curl of her lip.

'You are being unfair to her,' Gertie said when Mrs Keogh complained. 'She hasn't done anything wrong.'

'She talks too much. Far too friendly with the guests.'

'The guests are happy and the work gets done,' Gertie snapped. She suspected that Mrs Keogh also resented her friendship with Biddy.

Suddenly there was an influx of visitors and Biddy had to take on the extra task of chambermaid. She delivered breakfast each morning to those who had ordered it. Placing the tray brusquely on the bedside table and drawing the curtains with a whoosh, Biddy would call, 'Good morning,' in a cheerful voice.

'That time.' Mr Goodall, who had arrived the previous day from Huddersfield, stretched and rubbed his eyes.

'It's a beautiful day,' Biddy said, as she pulled the curtains, her back to the bed and Mr Goodall.

The lawn stretched out below, shadowy and silver with dew. A shaft of sunlight struck the low wall.

'Would you like me to pour your tea?'

'I don't feel very well.' Mr Goodall's voice was plaintive. 'Something I ate, I suspect.'

'You poor thing. The food here is rich.'

'That's the trouble. Hard to resist, like yourself.' He gave her a roguish smile, and felt better when he saw the look of concern on her face.

Biddy poured his tea, with one eye on the half-open door, in case she needed to make a hasty retreat. She handed him the steaming cup and said, 'Get out in the fresh air today. It'll do you good.'

He sipped the tea. 'Ah, that's better. You're right. I'll go for a walk. Would you like to come?' He grinned slyly at her.

'You're a devil, Mr Goodall. I've work to do.'

Biddy never spared herself. She had her home to keep clean for her mother, and the shopping to do sometimes. But this particular morning she felt sorry for Mr Goodall.

He looked vulnerable, as he lay there, grateful for her attention. He was a middle-aged, lonely man who had buried his wife the previous year.

She could hear voices downstairs. Someone calling her name.

'Jasus,' Biddy exclaimed. 'And not a bed made yet. I'd better go.' She vanished, cursing under her breath.

Biddy collected her mop and brushes, dustpan and dusters. She disappeared upstairs, away from the bedlam of the kitchen. 'Make sure you get into all the corners,' was all Gertie had ever said to her.

Later she walked jauntily to the clothes-line, the basket of washing bumping against her side. Pegging up the wet clothes, her hair shining in the sun, she smiled to herself. She loved the garden. As she dipped her strong arms into the washing basket, she was unaware of Mr Goodall peering out at her from behind the net curtains of his bedroom. Gertie's voice, calling John to take his shoes off, brought her back to reality. The sky was blue, clouds drifting hurriedly. She leaned against the wall for a minute, listening to the sound of a lawnmower in the distance, a motor car, the clop clop of Mr Meaney's horse's hooves heralding the milk delivery. The sound of steady noises soothed her, and reminded her of the safety of her childhood.

Biddy hung up the last of the washing and went to get the jug for the milk.

Mr Meaney's horse was waiting outside, flies buzzing around his ears, while Mr Meaney went from door to door.

'Two pints today, please, and Mrs Doyle says will you dip the milk.'

'Does she now?' Mr Meaney gave her a caustic look. 'I bet it's the freshest milk those foreigners ever tasted. They drink enough of it.' Mr Meaney plunged the long-handled ladle deep and started filling the jug.

'Can't be careful enough,' Biddy said.

'Don't like suspicious customers,' Mr Meaney muttered as Biddy walked away.

The house was quiet, the visitors gone to see the Book of Kells, or Glendalough, or perhaps the Zoo. It was the time of day Biddy liked the best. Mrs Keogh had gone for the messages, so there was only Gertie and herself. Gertie made a cup of tea for them both and read out Lizzie's letter.

Lizzie was employed at Flushing Hospital in New York. The war was over and America's industry was thriving. Workers of every age, colour and creed were being employed. Lizzie was a good nurse. She was positive and just in her dealings with everyone she came into contact with. Sometimes she was lonely, and in her loneliness she thought of home and her family:

'My walls are covered with scenes of Ireland,' she wrote, 'cut out of a calendar and hung in cheap frames.' Now on the verge of marriage, she felt that New York had matured her. 'It was here that I became a person in my own right, with possessions, responsibilities, experience and achievements. Pete is beginning to take an interest in the wedding plans. He's looking forward to seeing everybody again. And, needless to say, I'm looking forward to having you all here too. I can't tell you how much I miss you.'

'Huh,' Gertie said. 'She's giving New York all the credit. But does it make up for the homesickness?' With a sigh Gertie folded the letter and replaced it in the envelope ready for Bill to read. 'That's life,' she sighed. 'You rear them, put everything you have into them, and off they go and leave you with the memories.'

'You'll have a great time at the wedding,' Biddy said to cheer her up.

'I'm looking forward to it. But oh, how I miss her.'

Gertie was good to Biddy. Working for her made life less bleak, and the company of others gave her comfort.

Karen and John came up from the basement. As soon as they entered the house, the atmosphere changed. Everything became alive, more vivid.

Gertie hugged John. 'How was school?'

'OK. I'm starving.' He went straight into the kitchen and opened the cupboard where she kept the tins of cakes and biscuits.

'We had a maths test. I think I did well.'

'Of course you did.'

'He's always hungry,' Karen said.

'He's a growing lad. How's Paul?'

'Resting. He's seeing some new doctor from London next week.'

'You never know what the outcome might be.'

'I had a letter from Vicky.'

'Oh good. What did she say?'

Karen took a letter from her pocket, and sat down at the table to read it aloud.

'I'm busy keeping law and order in this hospital. Making the patients toe the line. God knows I don't envy them, and I suppose I should be more grateful for my health, which will suffer if we don't get shorter hours. We're working round the clock, but at least I'll be able to get time off soon. Carl and I are going to the Lakes for a few days. I'll have to swot though for the exams. We're all looking forward to Lizzie's wedding. Mum and Dad are coming too, but I'm hoping to travel separately. Can you imagine the journey to New York with the two of them jabbering all the way about the past? I've enclosed my measurements as requested. Something low and slinky would be nice for my bridesmaid's dress. Are you matron of honour?

It's exciting news about the guest-house. I wish I was there to meet all those people, though I don't think I'd like the work that's involved. Give Gertie and Bill my love and tell them I'm dying to see them again. Love to Paul and a big kiss for John. Dashing back to work.

Love Vicky'

'She must be nearly qualified.' Gertie took the letter to read it again.

'Only another year, and then it's Doctor Victoria Rosenblum.'

John ate as they talked. He delved into his schoolbag for pen and paper, and began his homework, impatient to get on with it so that he could go out to play. Gertie patted him proudly on the head. He was aware of her pride. Karen was a good mother, of that she was sure. But she had been distracted from the security of her marriage. Her serenity had been smashed when her husband Paul, a fighter pilot during the war, had gone missing in action. Without warning she had been tossed into a sea of fear, loneliness and pain from which she had never recovered.

John was one year old when Karen had left him with Gertie to return to England to try and find Paul. When all her efforts had failed, she became vague, and let Hank, Paul's cousin, run her life for her while she and John were in America visiting Paul's parents. From then on Hank had dictated her life. Then when Paul turned up after ten years, she had been lifted out of her inertia, and plunged into a state of ecstasy. Now she was fully occupied with Paul's recovery programme. Although John was the only constant in her life, he had been forced to take a back seat while Karen gave most of her attention to his father.

Gertie admired John's striving for independence. From the time Karen had returned to Ireland and left him with Bill and Gertie, while she trailed around Norway with Hank, he had come to her with questions that had no logical answers. 'Why did Mum leave me?' or 'Why did my daddy go away and never come back again?'

When Karen left him, he took it to heart. He was a serious boy, who suffered without too much complaint. Now that they were settled in Ireland again, Gertie felt that life for John would improve.

2

They slept three in a bed: Biddy on the outside because she was the eldest and therefore considered to be the bravest, Annie, who was ten, in the middle, and little May, who was only six, next to the wall. Their mother, Ita Plunkett, had told them that they were to be nice to one another and not fight; this was because their father was out of work, and the family had been threatened with eviction.

The possibility of eviction was a real terror in their lives. That their father could lose his job, and let them be evicted because he could no longer pay the rent was, their mother considered, criminal. Biddy's parents argued and shouted so much because of it that one day her father walked out the hall door, and did not return.

'Where will we go?' May asked.

Their mother pursed her lips. 'The only way from here is nowhere, and the worst of it is that I have no control over the matter. It's up to him.'

Later Biddy said in the quiet of their bedroom, 'Some day I'm going to own something of my own – something that nobody can take from me.'

'Like your own doll?' May asked.

'No, silly. I mean some place of my own to live in. Not like this dump either.'

Her eyes scanned the peeling brown wallpaper and the damp encrusted patches on the ceiling.

Biddy's house was a gloomy place; about a hundred years old, crouched at the end of a row of small terraced houses hidden behind the sea-front and the splendid facade of the Royal St George Yacht Club. The air was damp and chilly. They lived in the kitchen to keep warm. It had a stone floor, which Biddy swept regularly, a table and chairs, a rocking-chair by the fire, and a dresser with a few ornaments and plates on it. The other rooms were dark and cold. May imagined that they were peopled with ghosts in the dead of night.

Her mother had sad eyes and thin hair scraped back from her face, which gave her a severe look. Biddy thought her unreasonable when she shouted instructions at her, expecting her to carry them out without giving her any information.

One day soon after their father had left, May tripped and fell.

'God almighty!' her mother shouted. 'Can I not turn my back for a minute?'

Biddy refused to let her mother make her cry. She would see that as a sign of weakness. Guiltily she ran to pick up May. 'Is your knee sore?' she asked, as she wiped away May's tears. She put her arms around her and held her tight. 'Don't cry. Don't cry.' Biddy rocked her little sister.

'Bit late.' Their mother gave Biddy a look of disgust.

Biddy was full of remorse. At night in bed she tossed and turned, as the cold seeped up through the darkness into the cracks in the walls and frosted the window panes. May and Annie huddled into the corner of the bed. Biddy was wary of her mother's voice. She listened constantly for the inflection that signalled her mother was angry.

The mothers often congregated on the doorstep of one of the houses, their voices rising, falling and overlapping. Sometimes their voices sank with the depths of the emotions their tales invoked. Biddy watched from the open window as heads closed together. One day she saw her mother crying. One of the other women put her arms around her. Biddy's heart did a somersault. Then she heard her mother say, 'The disgrace of it all is that we have nowhere to go.'

Biddy missed her father. She used to like sitting by the fire listening to his stories, with the curtains drawn. His presence made her feel secure.

When the summer season was over and the visitors had all gone, Biddy's mother went to work for Doctor Gregory. Biddy had to stay at home to do the housekeeping. In the daytime she baked. The smell of newly baked bread cheered her up and, like the sound of the clock striking the hour, gave her life order and constancy. But her father's departure and the sound of her mother's crying interfered with her little pleasures.

She dreaded scrubbing the clothes in the big tub. The washboard grazed her knuckles, and her hands were red from squeezing clothes through the mangle. Chilblains, from pegging them on the clothes-line with wet hands, plagued her. She preferred collecting pig slop from the neighbours, and selling it to Mr Kelly, the slop-man. He drove a horse and cart up and down the streets of Dun Laoghaire, collecting pig swill.

Preparation for Sunday was something Biddy did not look forward to. She had to give May a bath on Saturday night. She scrubbed her in the tin bath in front of the fire, and made a lather with the carbolic soap to wash down her back. May liked to kick and splash.

'Stop,' Biddy would beg, 'the priest will kill you tomorrow if he finds out you were bold.'

May had a mental picture of the priest thumping the pulpit, crying out for sinners to repent and do penance. What was it about May that made their mother look at her with such gentleness? Although she was only six years old she seemed to possess a magic power over their mother.

What saved Biddy from anonymity was her position as the eldest. She was the one her mother depended on, the one she treated like an adult. Her mother never told anecdotes about Biddy's childhood because there was no time to remember it, or moon over it, as she did over May's. There were special recollections about May's babyhood, a sort of preferential treatment.

But there were compensations also. Biddy felt responsible. She also felt restricted. The loneliness would not go away. In her spare time she made dresses for May out of remnants her mother bought in McCullough's. May would have to stand still while Biddy pinned old newspapers on her and cut out the pattern.

Sometimes in the evenings she painted colours on big stones she had collected from the sea-front and brought home on the carrier of her bike. First she painted the stones white. According to their size and shape, she then painted scenery on them, working in small daubs with her index finger. She had a natural ability for combining colours. Her mother let her paint the stones, and then would arrange them neatly in the garden, between the rows of flowers. If somebody moved or tried to damage them, her mother would get angry.

Biddy did not mind the cooking and cleaning. She was good at it. What she did not like was the disruption at three o'clock, when Annie and May returned from school. Her peace was shattered. During her quiet time alone in the house, she fantasized about bettering herself: perhaps getting a job, and finishing school at night. Another fantasy was about Anthony Quinn, the leader of their gang.

Strange feelings washed over her when she thought of him, making her long to be near him. Anthony was strong and unafraid. He always knew what to do, which was why he was the leader of the gang. When Biddy was in his presence she acted differently. She laughed too much to conceal her anxiety. Sometimes she could not stop laughing, although she knew she was laughing at nothing. Sometimes he laughed with her, sending shivers down her spine, like the time she told him she wanted to be a singer, although she could not sing. She loved him, of that she was certain. Often love songs seeped through her, hinting at a promise of something to come. But Biddy was not sure how she should behave with him, or even how he should behave with her, and there was nobody she could ask.

When she met him in the fields, or outside the Workmen's Club or the cinema, her dreams came together. He talked to her, treated her as an equal, and sometimes singled her out from the rest of the gang. He liked telling her about himself and relished explaining things to her.

Nothing he did shattered her dreams, because he made her feel special. When she was with him, she felt that her poverty was not a disgrace, because he was also poor. It was something that would be rectified some day. When Gertie called to ask her mother if Biddy could help her out in the guest-house, her mother agreed because Annie was old enough to look after May.

For the first time since her father left, Biddy felt secure. Gertie appreciated her work and treated her like a member of the family. She would read out Lizzie's letters from America when the work was done and the house was quiet. Sometimes she would wait until Mrs Keogh had gone, and there were only the two of them.

At times like that Gertie would make a pot of tea and butter scones, all the time talking to Biddy about Gran, Lizzie and Vicky, the way things were, and her regret that Lizzie was not planning to return to Ireland.

When he went to London to train for the International Middleweight Boxing Championships, Anthony had stayed in a boarding house and was training for the fight. London seemed strange to him. His childhood summers had been spent following summer pursuits, like fishing and swimming, perhaps inventing a new game that could be performed outdoors.

He felt lonely walking along the bustling streets in the intense heat. For the first week he spoke to no one, apart from his landlady and his trainer. The others in his class, foreigners, were reticent. They were all serious young men. Most of them were obsessed with the fighting. They practised with fierce intensity, fighting one another under the supervision of the trainer, or frantically practising on a punching bag. Not once did they look at one another, or engage each other in conversation. Each one treated the other like an opponent at all times. If Anthony tried to catch the eye of one of them, or say something friendly, the trainer would glare at him.

Some of them were bigger and more skilled at boxing than Anthony, but they did not have his determination and nerve. He was always first to take a chance. He could climb a tree, swim across a lake, or fight lads older than him. Because he would not allow himself to lose, he was convinced that he would become a winner. There had to be something better than factories and building sites, and the feeling of rejection when he was refused a job. Money was to be made in boxing, and the Middleweight Championship was a rich prize in sport.

Anthony's trainer, Marty, was a sinewy man with light blue eyes and a broken nose. His hands were misshapen; a result of several hundred contests as a professional boxer. He was also a shrewd businessman who had managed fighters since his retirement from boxing and had organised matches for the International Boxing Club. Each day Marty walked around the room, stopping in front of one or other of the boys, to make sure that each one believed that he merited his singular attention.

'Anthony Quinn.' His voice was loud, commanding and made the boys jump.

'Yes, sir.'

'Step forward.'

Anthony stepped forward.

'Turn.'

Anthony turned.

'I want you in my office now.'

Quaking, Anthony followed him into his office.

Without inviting him to sit down, Marty said, 'Your body's soft. You must be getting fond of pasta. It's filled out your belly. Your fighting's crude, and you have no respect for the rules. Your legs are too thick, and you're not really tall enough.' He paused. Anthony's face was brick-red. 'But you can punch,' he continued, 'if crudely. And you have the will. We might make something of you yet.'

'Yes, sir.'

'We'll increase the training: more weightlifting and running on roads. And I'll speak to your landlady about your diet. Of course I expect your full co-operation.'

'Yes, sir.'

'Beginning tomorrow morning at six o'clock sharp, we'll run through Hyde Park, together.'

Anthony's room at the boarding house was bare and unwelcoming. In the evenings he ran through Hyde Park, or skipped in the narrow backyard, until the perspiration streamed down his face, while his landlady, Mrs Pavi, cooked spaghetti and meatballs. He hated spaghetti, and would sit twirling the slippery coils around his fork, trying to pick it up without making a mess. All the time he longed for a plate of bacon and cabbage, or floury potatoes, washed down with a pint of milk out of the bottle. Mrs Pavi only took in men, charging them a pound a week less if they shared a room. Mostly they came and went. Two of them were permanent, and friendly with one another.

Seán Cooney arrived from Liverpool one summer's evening. He was a tall man of about thirty, with a Northern Irish accent. He ate everything with relish.

'You're a powerful woman, Mrs P,' he would say when she placed his dinner in front of him.

She would smile with pleasure and sometimes produce wine. He was chatty and engaged them all in stories, most of which were littered with obscenities, after the evening meal. Sometimes he stayed out all night, and always had a good yarn to tell when he met up with them again at the next meal. Anthony began to look forward to the evenings, and often sat in the dining-room long after the evening meal was over, waiting for Seán to appear.

One Sunday morning while Anthony was finishing his breakfast, Seán came down, rubbing his eyes, and enquiring about breakfast.

'Breakfast is over,' Mrs Pavi said, indicating the tables still covered with egg-streaked plates, bits of bacon rind, and ground-out cigarette butts. When she saw the disappointment on his face, she said, 'I'll make you a bacon sandwich.'

Seán beamed at her. 'You're a star, Mrs P.'

'And you're a charmer.' She grinned with pleasure and began clearing the tables.

'Where is everybody?' Seán asked Anthony.

'Gone to Mass, the ones that worship,' Anthony said, just as the bells pealed out the quarter hour.

'I slept it out. Damn.'

Anthony laughed. 'I've never seen you up so early. What are you late for?'

Seán shrugged non-committally. 'I had arranged to meet someone. They'll be gone.' He glanced at his watch. 'What are you doing yourself?'

'Nothing much,' Anthony said, dreading the expected emptiness of the day.

'Want to come to the pub for a beer or something?'

'Wouldn't mind.'

Seán lowered his voice. 'I'll introduce you to a couple of pals of mine. Important blokes in the North.'

'In business?'

'No. In the IRA.'

'I didn't know the IRA was still in existence,' Anthony remarked.

'Not only is it in existence, it's flourishing.' The enthusiasm in Seán's voice surprised Anthony.

The pub that afternoon was dark and busy. Cigarette smoke hung in the air over the barman's head.

'Two pints of Guinness please,' Seán said to the barman. 'Not the same as the Irish Guinness.' He was eyeing the black drink as it rose in the glass. 'Only a martyr would drink it.'

The barman chuckled. 'All I can say is that the place must be full of martyrs.'

Seán placed the drinks on the table. Anthony took a sip of the creamy forth. 'How did you get involved?' he asked.

'Shh,' Seán cautioned. 'Don't want the whole place knowing about it. That would never do.'

Anthony blushed. 'Sorry.'

'Family influences I suppose. My mother was a dedicated Republican. She used to say that the only way to get the English off our soil was by force of arms. We don't consider it a crime to take arms against our enemies.'

Anthony pulled his chair up close to Seán's. 'Tell me more.'

'The aim of the Army is to drive the invader from the soil of Ireland and to restore the sovereign independent Republic proclaimed in 1916. To that end, the policy is to wage a successful military campaign against the British forces of occupation in the Six Counties.'

'How do you know all that?'

'It's my job to know it. I'm not a babe in arms.'

'They say things about that lot.'

'What things?'

'Are you one of them?'

Seán laughed. 'It's not as simple as that. They say things about everyone and everything. You don't want to listen to people. There's a lot of talk about getting the British out, but there's more to it than that.' His voice was low, his face angry.

'Are you active?' Anthony's voice was a whisper.

Seán nodded. 'Since I was eighteen. Running errands over the border. Living close to it was an advantage. And my motives were good. Set old Ireland free. You know what it's like when you're that age.'

The two paused and took a sip from their drinks.

'I like you, Anthony. You strike me as a bloke with guts. And you're strong. How's it going in the gym?'

'I can't please the coach no matter what I do. I wouldn't mind, but the mock fights are good.'

'Can I come and watch? I'll sit there, inconspicuous – one of the family.'

Anthony laughed. 'That'd be great. I'd like it if you did.'

'I'm off again soon.'

'Where?'

'Can't say. I'll keep in touch though.' Seán lowered his voice. 'You know we're always on the lookout for new blood.'

Anthony began, 'I'm not sure if . . .' but Seán would not let him finish.

'Think about it. Come on, finish your drink and we'll have a game of darts.'

Anthony missed Seán. Sometimes he went to the cinema. He would sit in the dark, comforted by the familiarity of the American scenes and accents, wondering how he would endure the next month without Biddy and the gang. Once he cried, thinking of her, wondering what she was doing. The thought that she might be enjoying herself without him was more than he could bear.

3

For Karen, the most straightforward plans were fraught with complications. She planned to take Paul to the Richmond, catching the 7A or 8 bus to Dublin. Then she would have a sandwich in the café near the hospital, and perhaps browse in the shops, while he was having his check-up. There was no subterfuge about that. Yet when Paul heard her idea, she was faced with objections and left feeling that she was fighting a losing battle.

'There's no need for you to go off. It won't take long.' Paul was sprawled on the sofa where he spent most of his time when she mentioned her plan to him. 'Why bother coming with me, if you're not going to stay and hear what they have to say?'

'It won't do any harm to leave you in the care of the nurses just this once.' She spoke calmly, knowing that to lose her patience would provoke an argument. 'It won't kill you.' She could have bitten off her tongue as soon as she had said it.

'Supposing they keep me in?'

'They'll let me know. Now I'd better get dinner ready.'

She left the room, closing the door behind her. Cold, rising from the cement floor in the passage, enveloped her, and she shivered. When they had first moved into the basement, she had assured her mother that she did not mind; she was young, she argued. But this evening she would have liked to have sat by the fire, rather than go out into the kitchen, feeling the draft in the passage which seeped in from the back door.

She and Paul had moved into the basement flat soon after their return to Ireland. It seemed to be the only way to ensure some privacy. At first everything went smoothly. The fact that Paul suffered from amnesia seemed to be accepted among their family and friends. People knew that Paul had gone missing in action during the war, and that they had not found him for ten years. Neighbours and friends treated him with respect, and kept a distance, not knowing how to approach him. Paul's parents sent him a lump sum of money. Karen bought furniture, and had a fireplace put into the front room, so they could use it as a sitting-room.

As time went on, the burden of Paul's medical expenses, keeping the place heated, providing food, all grew heavier and Karen wondered how she would manage. John was attending the local secondary school as a day pupil, and Karen had to pay the fees. But at least they were not paying rent, and she had her family upstairs to help with Paul, and to take an interest in John. She suspected that if she lived in a little house on the outskirts of town, nobody would care and she would be left to fade away into oblivion.

The kitchen was warm and the Aga cooker comforting. She remembered the time when the whole family had practically lived in the kitchen. Happy times, when Gran was alive, and they cooked, ate and entertained; they had even kept the sewing-machine there. Paul avoided the kitchen and, apart from meals, spent most of his time in their bedroom, or on the sitting-room sofa.

After dinner Karen went upstairs to ask Gertie if she would give John his dinner the next day while she and Paul were in Dublin.

Gertie was out shopping, and Mrs Keogh was cleaning the cooker, a chore guaranteed to put her in bad humour.

'How's Paul?' she asked.

'He's going for a check-up tomorrow.'

'He doesn't seem to be making much progress.'

Karen stiffened. 'There's a doctor over from London that they're anxious for him to see. Apparently he has some new ideas for patients like Paul.'

'He came on so well in the beginning, with his speech and everything.'

Karen knew that Mrs Keogh liked nothing better than to talk about illness.

'I heard of a man who was shot in the war and the bullet was lodged in his brain for the duration. Would you believe that he made a full recovery, and is working in the coal mines in Yorkshire now?'

'If only we knew where Paul was during the war. He just remembers snatches of it. If we could find out what happened to him . . .'

'Has anyone ever thought of giving him a good shake? That always worked with my Trevor when he forgot his lessons.'

'He's not a child.'

'All men are children in disguise,' Mrs Keogh said unsympathetically. 'You watch your own health. I see you running around after him, and him expecting it. You're a bundle of nerves. You wouldn't think of putting him in hospital, to give yourself a bit of a rest for a while?'

'No.'

'It's such a strain.'

'Paul is making a good recovery.'

Mrs Keogh had her own opinion of Paul. Not that she saw much of him these days. He kept himself hidden in the basement, which was just as well for everybody's sake. She thought he was a strange man, with an unnerving way of looking at her.

'He's as strong as an ox,' Mrs Keogh continued, more to herself than to Karen.

'His physical health is not the issue.'

'More's the pity. All that wasted strength. He could be out to work, earning enough money to keep you and John, and spare you from all the worry.'

Karen was outraged at the offensiveness of that remark. She wanted to tell Mrs Keogh to mind her own business, but she knew that her mother needed her to help run the guest-house.

'Paul's getting better. He'll work again when he's able.' Her voice was croaky with the strain of keeping herself in check.

Mrs Keogh gave a snort. 'I wouldn't count on it if I were you. One could get used to the life he has — being waited on hand and foot. You should look after yourself. Look at you — losing your looks. You could do with a trip to the hairdresser's. No man is worth it. Not even your precious Paul.'

'Mrs Keogh' Karen's voice was shaking, 'I came up to ask Mam to keep an eye on John, not to discuss Paul's health.' She was thinking, *I hate you, you interfering old battle-axe.*

'I was only taking an interest. It'd be something else if I didn't enquire. I'm worried about Gertie too. Slaving away to make money to go to New York. Wouldn't you think that Lizzie would come home for something as important as her own wedding?'

'Pete doesn't want to come back.'

'Typical. I'm surprised at Lizzie. She should put her foot down. After all, it's her day.'

'And it's her business.' Pulling herself together with extreme effort, Karen said, 'There's a chance that this doctor might be able to do something for Paul. If you could ask Mam to make sure John gets his dinner, I'd be grateful.'

'I'll make sure myself.'

'Thank you,' Karen said and left.

Back downstairs she sat in an armchair facing Paul, who was reading. Paul was thirty-five, but he looked older, more because of the permanent strain on his face than his grey hair. Yet he was immaculately dressed in tweed trousers and an Aran jumper, and seemed like someone in complete control.

Karen began hesitantly. 'I was thinking I might get a job.' Paul removed his horn-rimmed glasses, and gave her a cagey look. 'What for?'

'It's not easy to keep things going.'

'John needs you to be here when he comes home from school.'

'You could look after him for an hour or so.'

Paul looked into the fire. Eventually he said, 'I don't know what you're getting so worked up about. We're managing fine.'

'I'm not getting worked up.'

It was true that Paul's parents had sent them money, but it was not enough. They had no idea of the cost of living in Ireland. She also knew that Hank controlled the family estate in North Carolina. Even if Paul got better, she suspected that Hank would find some reason to deprive him of the estate that was rightfully his.

'Perhaps it isn't the money. Perhaps you're bored with being at home all day long,' Paul said. He was looking at her, expecting her to say something. She did not want to tell him about the doctors' bills.

Paul stood up, and went to revive the fire. 'Let us suppose

that this doctor can do something for me, though I don't hold out much hope. What happens if my memory is fully revived, and I can't live with the past hurts? Supposing I were to become some sort of monster? That is a far greater worry than the household bills.'

'Don't talk like that. I don't think I could bear it if you were to suffer any more.'

'I don't know if I want any more intrusion into my life by those doctors.'

'You won't get better until you let someone or something jog your memory and unlock your past.'

'I don't suppose we should make any constructive suggestions about the future until we see this doctor tomorrow. After all, we've been disappointed in the past.'

Karen knew by his demeanour that the conversation was over. She felt depressed. Finally she left the room, closing the door firmly behind her, and deciding to have a bath to calm herself, she lit the geyser suspended over the tub. Soon she was lying in the hot water, scented by the bubble-bath that John had given her for Christmas.

She lay there evaluating her life. Her initial euphoria at finding Paul had been replaced by exhaustion because of her constant care of him. She had devoted herself to his needs and the tasks his illness enforced upon her, almost to the exclusion of everything else. Gertie and Bill were determined not to interfere and Karen was content in her self-imposed isolation, glad to have Paul to herself.

As she considered her plight, she longed for a word of appreciation from Paul, although she knew he was incapable of expressing himself, at the moment anyway. Would things change? Would he ever hold her in his arms as he had once done, or hug her and tell her that she was wonderful? A little physical contact would do; anything to denote that she was not wasting her time. She wasn't even sure if he was where he wanted to be. How could she be when he did not know himself?

Only now did she realize why her family had been a little cautious when Paul was discovered. She remembered the worry in Gran's eyes. If only Gran were alive, Karen thought, she would confide in her as she did in the old days when her mother did not seem to understand her. Gran had spoiled Karen because she was her first grandchild. When Karen had spent her holidays with Gran in Limerick, she used to take her shopping to buy lace and crochet threads. She also bought the finest muslin to make her pretty smocked dresses, and afterwards there would be lemonade and cakes, sometimes chocolate treats that Gertie considered bad for Karen.

'Don't tell your mother,' Gran would say.

Karen remembered her wedding, when Gran had made the cake. Then she had smoothed over the arguments incurred by the decision to have a traditional white wedding, in spite of the fact that she was pregnant. If Gran feared the neighbours, she never said and was a tower of strength to Gertie when Karen walked down the aisle. Nor did anyone pass one disparaging remark at the reception in the Royal Marine Hotel. They would not dare in Gran's hearing.

She closed her eyes to recall her grandmother. A dapper lady in her eighties, with sharp eyes that missed nothing, and an endearing smile that was both affectionate and forgiving.

Gran had been born in County Limerick, ten miles from the city, and within two miles of the nearest village. Her parents had a neat cottage on a small farm where they reared their ten children. Her mother stole a patch of ground from the chicken runs out the back, and planted a border of flowers under the kitchen window, and another one at the front of the cottage.

Gran was the youngest child. Some of her brothers were living in America by the time she was born, one sister was a nun, and another had got married. The brothers sent home dollars and parcels of American clothes, which gave the family a feeling of security.

When Gran was old enough to leave school, her father made her stay at home to help out on the farm. She boiled huge pots of potatoes to feed the animals, collected eggs, drew water from the well, made bread – an old flour sack tied around her waist, men's boots on her feet. Gran was good at her work, but she hated it, and resented her father for not letting her stay on at school.

That was how her husband to be came across her one hot sunny day. Extra labour had been taken on for the threshing, and he was one of the strong young men who hired themselves out to neighbouring farms.

Gran, a long thick plait of hair down her back, was feeding the hens when she heard a low whistle. She turned around to find him, naked to the waist, looking at her.

'It's a thirsty day,' he had said. 'Any chance of a drink of water?'

The laughter in his eyes had captivated her.

'It was a hot day,' she often recalled. 'I could feel my hands wet on the handle of the bucket of meal, and my long cotton skirt was stuck to my legs. The men had been in the fields all day long, miles away, and the rest of the family were over in my Aunt Kate's having a little holiday. My mother and I had time to sit and talk while we did the mending. We picked wild flowers and decorated the house. It was the only time in my life I had my mother to myself.'

In the years to come Gran often talked about that first year of knowing one another.

'Johnny loved me then,' she used to say. 'He liked being with me; liked my funny ways, my superstitions, and he didn't care about my lack of book-learning. He made me laugh,' she would add in wonderment.

They were young, enthusiastic and in love when they married and settled down a year later, on his father's smallholding thirty miles from the Limerick–Cork border.

'We were happy at first: me home. Johnny working on the land. Then his father died and he was gone all day, and sometimes into the night. There were no houses nearby, and when he was too tired to talk, and I was too pregnant.

Karen lay back in the hot water. Gran's life had not been an easy one, but she had never questioned God's motives, especially when her husband had died young, leaving her to fend for her five young children. And children were important to her. Karen and Lizzie were her favourite grandchildren until Vicky arrived from war-torn England with her cardboard suitcase and gas mask. Gran took charge of her, and Lizzie was jealous. Karen remembered Lizzie telling her how Vicky and she had trudged down to the Roman Café for ice-cream, in their skimpy sun-dresses, their faces a concentration of importance.

The Roman Café, where young people could sit and gossip, was in the centre of Dun Laoghaire. Boys huddled around the door watching girls enter and leave. They would snigger, comment, or whistle at the retreating young girls. Lizzie would nudge Vicky to keep going, and shield her own face with her tumbling hair. Vicky would wink at the boys sometimes, or stick her tongue out, to Lizzie's great embarrassment. It was not the ice-cream that made Lizzie endure that moment of torture when she was never sure of Vicky's reaction to those boys. Or the grown-up feeling of having money to spend. It was the excitement that the close proximity of the boys aroused in both of them. The thrill of the knowing smiles, the meaningful glances, the slight movement of hip or thigh that could plunge them into a dreamlike state, and keep them in conversation for days, perhaps weeks on end.

Vicky was an only child, a lonely little girl who had endured endless hours in the London air raids waiting for her mother's return. Gran had told Karen that when Vicky had first arrived in Dun Laoghaire, she was watchful and distrusting. It took Gran's sympathetic eyes, soothing words and the comfort of her arms to give her confidence.

Lizzie, too, was a solitary child. Karen, Lizzie's only sister, was ten years older and lived away from home. With the arrival of Gran, the house became chaotic. Gran had a tendency to slam doors and raise her voice, and although Lizzie swore that she loved Gran living with them, Lizzie had no companion her own age. As far as Gran was concerned the coming together of Vicky and Lizzie was fortunate for them both. Soon they felt at ease with one another. Their friendship was intense, often exploding into rows which could cause rifts that Vicky would sustain until Gran wore her down, or she needed Lizzie for something or other. Lizzie was stronger and more emotionally consistent, and if it appeared that Vicky was the leader, it was not true, Gran often said.

Vicky went on to study medicine at the University of Toronto. She often wrote to Gertie and Bill, and occasionally to Karen. In her letters she told them what a struggle it was for women practising medicine. Her role was seen as one of defiance by some. She had always been that way. 'I realize that I'm luckier than most women because I'm attractive, and I accept the fact that men like me and want to please me,' she wrote to Karen. Quick to comment when something was inefficient, or not to her satisfaction, she soon won the respect of her fellow students.

It seemed to Vicky, according to her letters, that she had spent most of her life studying, working harder than everybody else to be the best in her class, because she could never settle for anything less. Whether her ambition stemmed from her secret desperation to meet with her father Hermy's approval, or her own determination to make something of her life so that she would be valued for herself, she was not sure. But her studying had paid off with grades that had ensured her a place in medical school.

In her first year there was practical work in the hospital; examinations, blending in, drinking endless cups of coffee with other students, and eating cream cakes while discussing their futures. During those conversations their eyes would be full of hope and ambition. And sometimes mischief.

Now that she was almost qualified Vicky was no stranger to work. The only time she had ever taken off was when her mother had had a heart attack and she had gone to London for two months to take care of her. She was always afraid of having time on her hands, of not feeling useful or needed by someone. It was only on reflection that she realised how strong her ambition was.

Gran had understood Vicky's ambition, and had also understood the rivalry between herself and Lizzie. When Vicky went to Canada, that rivalry stopped, and the layers of resentment and jealousy between them disappeared. They became firm friends.

Now, Karen could not imagine Lizzie's wedding without Gran. Gran would have been the first member of the family to board the aeroplane, and the one to take charge and organize everything. Life was not the same without her.

4

It was late morning when Patsy Quinn woke up. She lay in her own bedroom, the smallest room in the house, admiring the curtains her mother had made to match the new bedspread. Although the Quinn family had been living in Sallynoggin for the past eighteen months, Patsy still sighed with pleasure at the thought of her family having a home of their own.

There were three bedrooms and a bathroom upstairs, a kitchen and a separate living-room downstairs. That room was wallpapered in a rosebud design, and the kitchen was painted white. The floors in the house were covered in brown linoleum, and Mrs Quinn was making a rug in pink wool to match the wallpaper.

Thirty of the new houses in Sallynoggin were occupied. The Quinns' was the last one to be finished in that particular row. The road ended outside their house, and a new road had been dug up and marked out. Gardens were fenced off with wire meshing, and Betty Quinn had to pick her way through hardened cement, rubble and bits of brick to get to the clothes-line. Damien, Patsy's three-year-old brother, was forbidden to play in the back garden. Sometimes Betty would let him play out in the front, on the bit of road that was completed, provided he stayed away from the building site and the half-finished houses opposite their own.

There were fields behind the houses and further up walls of bricks were lined in readiness for the building of the shops. A huge trench, in the middle of a field, was the foundation for the church. It had been cordoned off, but children played all around it, running and chasing in the freedom of the long grass. The Dublin mountains loomed bleak and magnificent in the distance.

Betty Quinn tried to imagine what rows and rows of houses would look like, piled into those bare fields, but she couldn't. She was too happy to care. Even when Damien trailed mud all over her floor, she did not chastise him. She would get down on her hands and knees and lovingly wash and polish every square inch of it. Sometimes he tripped on the road, skinning his knees, and bits of spiky cement had to be removed from his raw flesh before she could wash the blood off. She did not despair. Instead, she cajoled him with a spearmint bar, and let him out to play again.

The sun shone into the kitchen from the window behind Patsy's chair, warming her as she finished her breakfast of porridge and milk. Her mother moved around the kitchen with Brian, the baby, straddling her hip. She was a strong woman, although Patsy noticed that her back was slightly stooped.

'Here you are. Take him for a bit.' She put the baby in Patsy's arms. 'Good job you like babies.' She smiled at Brian, saying, 'Don't start,' as he began to whimper. Damien was bright-eyed and cheerful, and was content to lean against Patsy and suck his thumb.

The doorbell rang. When Damien saw that it was John, he leaped off his chair, and hurled himself at him.

'John, John, can we go blackberry-picking?'

'Let him get in the door, for God's sake.' Betty grabbed Damien, and led him back to the table.

'That's what I came for,' John laughed. 'Gertie wants to make blackberry jam, and I told her the juiciest ones were in the fields around here.'

'Great.' Patsy put Brian back in his pram. 'I'll get some bowls.'

'It's a lovely day,' Betty said. 'The fresh air should do Brian good.'

While John and Patsy picked blackberries, Damien played in and out of the ruts the builders had dug for foundations for the new houses. Brian slept in his pram, a half-empty bottle in his mouth. Birds sang in nearby bushes and faint voices of children could be heard. Patsy went to see who they were, and saw a cluster of caravans parked a distance away.

'Come and see,' she called to John.

'When did they get here?'

'I don't know, but I'd love to see what the inside of one of those caravans looks like.'

'Let's go down.'

John pushed the pram and Patsy followed, Damien's hand held tightly in one hand, the bowl of blackberries in the other. As they drew near the encampment, dogs barked and strained against the ropes that tied them to a fence. A black pot sat on a smouldering turf fire at the entrance, and washing was spread out on the hedgerow. Two raggy boys, brandishing sticks, stared at them with hostile eyes.

A stout woman, washing clothes in a big tub near one of the caravans, saw them approach and shouted to the boys to put down their sticks and say hello to the 'strange children'.

The caravans were painted green and yellow, their graceful curves bordered in red. John lingered to look in through the open door of one of them. Brass ornaments and flowery curtains were all he could see, before one of the boys shouted, 'Wha' are ye lookin' ah?'

He stared back at the bold-eyed boy, suddenly envious of his freedom. 'Would you like to play with us?' he called out to him, as Patsy pulled his sleeve to coax him away.

The boy, surprised by the invitation, was left speechless. He looked at them, then looked quickly away, too shy to meet their gaze. The dogs barked louder. The gypsy woman came over to them. 'What's your names?' Her soft brown eyes looked from one to the other.

'Patsy Quinn and Damien Quinn,' Patsy said, and John added, 'John Thornton.'

'What a bonny baby. Come 'ere Ginger, Geoff. Look at this beautiful babby.'

Her gold earrings twinkled in the sunlight as she tickled Brian, who screeched with laughter.

The boys stared sullenly at the baby.

'We can't stay out too long,' Patsy began.

'Come and play for a little while. We won't be here much longer.' Her voice was soft. 'I'll mind the baby.'

A man appeared at the door of one of the caravans. He wore an old, open-necked shirt and brown trousers. His boots were worn and dirty.

'Ye're a desperate woman Mag,' he said. 'Haven't you enough to be doin'?'

'Ah, but look at the babby.'

The children eyed him.

'Hello,' he called.

They answered 'hello' in unison and he disappeared inside.

'What'll we play?' John asked the boys, who were about ten.

They shifted from one foot to another, then one of them said, 'Anythin' at all. We don't mind.'

They played tag and threw stones into the river, then splashed one another with water carried from the stream in a tin can full of tiny holes.

'Come and see our pony,' Geoff said, leading them behind the caravans, where a piebald pony was tethered to an old iron bedhead.

'Snowball.'

The pony came to them. Geoff held him, while Ginger mounted.

'Giddy-up.' A flick of his heels against the pony's flanks sent him trotting off down the field. Fascinated, the children watched them disappear behind a clump of trees.

'Can I have a go?' Damien asked Patsy just as the woman called them over to the fire.

'Stay for a bit of stew,' she added, coaxing the embers into a bright flame.

'Smells delicious.' Patsy suddenly felt hungry.

'The table's laid,' she said. 'Come on in.'

She took them into one of the caravans. The man they had seen at the door was sitting at the table.

'Ye from the new houses?' His eyes gleamed in his narrow face, they frightened Patsy.

'Yes, sir,' she replied, sitting down so as not to be conspicuous.

The woman went out, took the black pot from the fire and put it on the ground. Steam rose in a cloud as she lifted the lid. John licked his lips as she brought a bowl of hot stew to the table. The man cut lumps of crusty bread.

'For dippin' in.'

He motioned to John to take some. 'Pity ye have to come and eat our food. Have ye none of yer own?' He rocked with laughter, and Patsy suddenly felt ashamed and angry with herself for agreeing to stay. Damien sat on Patsy's knee and the woman held Brian, who fell asleep before they were finished.

'This is delicious.' John sank his spoon into the bowl to scrape up all the gravy.

'We got a nice bit of lamb in Fermoy a couple of days ago,' the man said.

'Where is that?' Patsy asked.

'Cork. We've travelled a lot in the past week. We're goin' to a weddin' in Arklow tomorrow. You boys are havin' a bath as soon as ye're finished yer supper.'

'Yuk.' Geoff made a hideous face.

'Where's Ginger?' the man asked and the woman went to the door.

Putting two fingers into her mouth, she whistled. The sound rent the air, and was echoed by another distant whistle.

'He's comin'.'

She sat down again. A few minutes later Ginger returned and tethered the pony to the door of the caravan.

The woman's eyes narrowed as he sat down at the table.

'You need a wash.'

She examined Ginger's ears. Ginger squirmed.

Patsy laughed.

'Eat up, it'll be time to go home soon,' the man said. 'I'll get the bath.' He went out to the back of the caravan and returned with an aluminium bath. Geoff and Ginger kicked off their shoes and hopped around the fire.

'Who lives in the caravan over there?' John asked.

'The rest of the family,' the woman replied, pouring water from a bucket into the bath. 'They're gone to the horse fair in Bray, they'll be back before dark.'

'We'd better go,' John said.

'Yeh. Before youse get washed and all,' shouted Geoff, who was peeling off his jumper.

The woman hugged each of them in turn. Her body felt warm and soft and John was reluctant to go. As they left, she was scrubbing the back of the naked Geoff, the soapy water running through her fingers.

The fields were dark and gloomy, and shadows drew in around them. As they made their way home, Damien began to cry. Patsy soothed him by telling him a story.

Betty Quinn was at the front door when they returned.

'In the name of God what kept you? You were gone all day! I was worried sick.' She lifted Brian out of the pram.

'We met some friends,' Patsy said. 'They asked us to stay to tea.'

'What friends?'

'Gypsies.'

'Gypsies. Don't they have enough children of their own? I hope you didn't eat their food.'

'I want to go back tomorrow,' Damien said.

'The only place you're going is to bed. Take him upstairs 'til I wash him, and John, you had better go home before it gets too dark.'

'I'll get the bus. It should be here in a few minutes.'

'I'll see you on Monday,' Patsy called over her shoulder, as she hauled a reluctant Damien up the stairs.

★ ★ ★

Bob Quinn came home from work and ate his evening meal silently. The fact that he had provided the meat from the butcher's shop he worked in seemed to give him extra authority in the evenings, and Patsy was in awe of him. When he had finished eating, he said to Betty, 'George Johnson was in today. Bought three pounds of my best sirloin steak. He's looking for someone to help with the cleaning and cooking.'

'Is his wife sick again?'

'Pregnant.'

'That makes it nine, and she's not strong, poor woman.'

'He'll pay the top price. I told him I'd ask you—'

'Me? Haven't I enough to do here?'

'I'm the one who has to provide for you all. Everyone in this house is dependent on me; I have to keep working so that the rest of you can sit at home drinking tea all day.'

'Mammy's always working,' Patsy piped up.

'There's a lot to be done.'

'Then why don't you help more? You're big and strong now, and well able. Or leave school and get a job yourself.'

'Bob.' Betty said his name in a placatory way. 'Patsy's too young to leave school. And she's clever. Sister Martin wants to enter her for the scholarship for the secondary school.'

'More of your high notions.' He dropped his knife and fork on the plate, stood up, and marched out of the room. 'You're all expecting too much from me, the one pair of hands, the only breadwinner.'

The front door banged.

'I hate the way he shouts at you.' Patsy looked sympathetically at her mother.

'He'll calm down. He doesn't mean any harm. It's over now anyway.'

But it was not over. Patsy knew that was the mistake her mother always made.

The next morning Karen was urging John to hurry up and eat his breakfast, while she made him his favourite ham sandwiches and boiled up the kettle for his flask of tea. Paul finally came into the kitchen, dressed in his good suit.

'Why can't I go with you?' John asked.

'Next time.'

Paul began eating the rashers and sausages Karen had placed in front of him. She looked at the clock. 'Hurry up. It's time to go,' she said, getting John his coat.

'But I'm not finished my breakfast . . .'

She was not listening.

Finally she rushed him out the door.

In their bedroom she sat at her dressing-table. She would have liked to have looked her best, but there was not time for mascara and rouge. With a quick flick of her powder puff, and the run of a comb through her hair, she was ready.

She and Paul walked in silence to the bus stop. The bus trundled along, stopping every few minutes. It made for a long journey. Karen gazed out of the window, wondering how many more trips like this they would undertake, and if they would be worthwhile. She was remembering the more pleasurable trips to Dublin, with Gran, when she used to come to Dublin from Limerick to do her Christmas shopping. If only she could wave a magic wand and revert to those days.

Karen's thoughts turned to Lizzie's wedding. Where would they get the money to go? How would Paul manage the journey? They would have to visit his family, who were anxious to see him while they were in America.

A picture of Gran came into Karen's mind: old, shaky, growing frail, leaning on her stick. Gran at the station kissing her good-bye when she was leaving for England, her bony fingers gripping Karen's hand, her white head bent to brush away a tear. Then reaching up to grab her, for one last hug, before the whistle blew. Her arms waving as the train pulled away, her tiny frame becoming enveloped in a swirl of vapour. Karen could still picture her hand waving, and Gran growing smaller and more distant as the train gathered speed.

5

Although his opponent was a taller and a heavier man, Anthony was favoured by the judges. Oblivious to pain, he could absorb any amount of punches before delivering his own. At the end of the fourth round, his opponent had to retreat. A left hook put him down in the next round, and though he was up at the count of six, it was not long before there were signs of trouble as Anthony renewed his assault.

Anthony, with eyes vacant, legs quivering, drove him to the ropes, where he dealt him another savage hook. But his opponent retaliated with a chilling right, which ripped Anthony's jaw. He fell backwards. He was down for the first time for the count of three.

His opponent expected him to withdraw from a predictable onslaught. Instead, Anthony came back, throwing punches with both hands. In a minute of frenzied activity, he landed a left hook and his challenger went over.

Blazing with indignation, Anthony launched savage counter-attacks. Each time Anthony returned to his corner, his handlers expressed their anxiety, while attempting to staunch the gaping wounds.

By the end of the fifth round Anthony was a mess, with blood seeping from cuts around his eyes, and his lips.

'You're losing,' Marty said. 'You'll have to knock him out. Come on, you can do it.'

'I'll pulverize him,' Anthony said.

He returned to the centre of the ring, and delivered a short right with such force that his opponent's face suddenly became a mask of blood. As the other boxer crumpled Anthony punched him hard in the lower ribs. He sank to one knee, his left arm hooked around the middle rope, his head resting on the canvas. The referee began to count. The bout was over. Anthony's rough-house tactics had led to his instant disqualification.

'What'll happen now?' Anthony asked Marty, as he anxiously watched his opponent being carried out on a stretcher.

'Depends on whether the poor chap pulls through or not. You fought dirty.'

'He hit me low, so I hit him lower.'

'You went too far this time. You were out of line.'

Marty looked at the bruised and cut spectacle before him. 'I'll say one thing for you though. You have a fighting spirit.'

'Could be my downfall.'

'We'll have to wait and see what the Control Board say.'

Seán was waiting outside. 'You were unfortunate.' He put his arm around Anthony's shoulder.

'I didn't realize I hit him so low.'

'You're a bit battered yourself. Brawling comes naturally to you, Anthony.'

'Looks like there won't be any more fights for a while. Marty says it could be a long wait.'

'I think I could get you fixed up in a job while you're waiting.'

The pieces of Anthony's life that had become coherent to him had suddenly begun to fall apart. He felt that nobody could ever understand that the boxing had given true form to his life. Now that gift could be taken away with one fight in London; one blow in a fit of temper.

He had seen the anger in the eyes of the referee, saw his opponent's manager gesturing in a quarrelsome, agitated manner with Mr Murphy, their faces angry. Anthony noticed, through bruised eyes, the closed-off expression on Mr Murphy's face as they left the hotel. Mr Murphy, that giant of a man, was suddenly no taller than the other angry men who surrounded him. His expression was no different from the belligerent faces of the other men.

Anthony returned from London and was quiet – talking only in monosyllables. He refused to give Biddy any details about the fight, and when his pals questioned him he cut their conversations short. He would sit hunched over the counter in Mooney's pub reciting how many pints he had drunk, to the anticipated praise of his friends, Reilly and Spud.

The judges' decision depended on the state of his opponent's health, and Anthony worried that it might take a long time. When he did talk, his conversations were empty and shapeless.

One evening, shortly after his return, Biddy said to him, 'I don't know what you hope to gain from your stupid carry-on. I'm the only one who cares. The others are sick of you.'

'Who asked you for your opinion anyway?' he shouted, walking away.

Most evenings he staggered home drunk, but not too drunk to see the despair in his mother's eyes. She would be hunched over a sinkful of dirty dishes, or a bathtub of washing, her hands submerged in soapy water, her face shining with perspiration.

'It mightn't be all that bad,' she would offer by way of comfort, but Anthony felt only pity for her, and hopelessness for himself.

Biddy made him uncomfortable, looking at him, head to one side, eyes haunted by unanswered questions.

'What do you want me to do? What do you want me to say?' he would ask, and then look away.

'Say anything, only say something,' she would answer, her misery an accusation.

He wanted to tell her that he loved her, that what had happened in the boxing ring had nothing to do with her. But he felt useless. If the boxing were to be taken away from him, he had nothing left to give her. What could he accomplish with his limited background that would be deserving of her love? Biddy, a pretty, smiling girl who found joy in life, who wanted to make something of herself, would grow to dislike him.

Resentment rose up in him for her relentless interference in his life. He wanted to be left alone to wallow in self-pity, and that feeling of gloom relieved his guilty conscience.

One day when they were coming out of the Adelphi Cinema, Biddy linked his arm and asked him if he loved her. When he pretended not to hear her question, she turned to him and said, 'I'm off.'

She walked away, hurrying down the street, hair flying in the cold wind.

Spud, Reilly, Banger and Anthony stood huddled together at the corner fastidiously smoking cigarettes, occasionally spitting into the gutter. Anthony inhaled his Woodbine deeply, filling his lungs with smoke. That seemed to give him satisfaction. Jittery with excessive energy, he ground the butt into the pavement and said, 'Let's do something.'

'What?' Reilly asked.

'Rob a bank.'

Banger shivered. 'I haven't got the nerve. Let's go for a drink.'

'I've got a few deliveries to make,' Spud said. 'Anyone coming with me?'

'We'll do the deliveries, and then we'll go for a pint.' Anthony looked from one to the other.

'You're on,' they said in unison, and moved off slowly, as if they were putting some secret plan into action.

They arrived at the Purty Kitchen at ten o'clock. Like all pubs it was busy with customers sitting in groups at tables, or hunched together at the bar. The barman poured beer and Guinness into pint glasses, and placed them carefully on the counter. He spotted Anthony.

'Howayah?' he called out. 'Haven't seen you for ages. How was the fight?'

Anthony barely responded.

'Boxing isn't the same,' the man standing next to Anthony said. 'The only good ones are the blacks.'

Anthony slammed his glass on the counter. 'Fill that up Mick,' he said to the bartender.

The man leaned forward. 'It's a black man's game. How could you expect to compete against them? They're the best.'

'What do you mean?' Spud said.

'They move differently. Better trained. More agile.'

Anthony ignored him.

He began naming them: 'Sugar Ray Robinson, Archie Moore . . . the game's changed anyway. It was better in my time.'

Anthony turned to him. 'You think the game was better in your time? Come on then. Let's see how you did it.' He smiled pleasantly at him.

Awareness slowly dawned on the other man's face.

Anthony bunched his fists.

The barman lurched forward, reaching out to grab Anthony's arm. 'This is not the place for a fight, and you've got drink taken. If you want to continue this, find a public venue.'

The other man looked grateful.

Anthony got to his feet. The others followed him silently.

When he returned home, the house was silent. He removed his shoes and tiptoed upstairs. Quietly he took off his clothes and got into bed. The sheets were cold.

He stayed in bed late the next day, and went out in the evening before his father came home, to avoid him. But he knew he was being watched, and no matter how much his mother defended him, his father was waiting to catch him out.

He went for walks, helped Spud in the shop, and spent the money Spud paid him on drink. When the silence got him down, he would walk the dark deserted streets. His room was a mess and smelled of sweat and beer.

The next evening the doorbell rang. Biddy was standing in the doorway, in a new yellow dress. Her hair was tied back in a ponytail, and she was smiling.

'Are you going to ask me in?'

He could smell her perfume as she passed him in the hallway.

'Where's everyone?'

'Don't know. Out, I suppose.'

'Will you come to the Arcadia ballroom tonight? We're all going.' She spoke in a rush.

'Who's we?'

'Everyone.'

'Don't think so.'

'Why?'

'Don't feel like it.'

'Do you know what, Anthony Quinn?'

'What?'

'You're enjoying your misery. Do you realize that? In some perverse way, you're enjoying all this. Everyone's worried about you. And it makes you feel good. Well, you can count me out. I'm off.'

She spun around and went back out the front door.

'Biddy, wait.'

She was gone, walking down the road, her yellow dirndl skirt swirling around her legs.

The next day Anthony called to her house. She looked at him guardedly. 'What do you want?'

'Don't be like that.'

'Like what?'

'Can I come in?'

'I don't want any scenes.' In the kitchen, clothes were scattered here and there. The ironing-board stood in the middle of the floor.

'Do you want a cup of tea?'

'No, thanks. Come out with me. I want to talk to you.'

'Wait a few minutes 'til I tidy up.'

They walked down to the sea-front, and along the path to Sandycove. The sea was calm, ruffled only by a cool breeze. Biddy took off her shoes and socks and waded slowly into the water.

'It's lovely. Come on in.'

'Are you mad? It's too cold.'

'Coward.' She pulled her skirt up around her thighs, and waded out further.

Anthony thought she looked beautiful.

When Biddy came out they sat side by side on the sea wall.

'I'm sorry I shouted at you yesterday,' she said, 'but I don't know what's got into you. I can't understand you any more.'

He gave her a quick kiss on the lips. 'I've got a job.'

'Where?'

'I can't tell you. The fella who arranged it for me told me not to say anything, until things are more definite.'

'Doing what?'

'Working on building sites. Bit of everything I suppose.'

'Here?'

'No.'

Biddy looked straight ahead. 'So you'll be off again?'

'Yes.'

'When?' She could feel the tension in her own voice.

'Soon as I've heard from my friend. It might take a few weeks.'

'What about Mr Murphy?'

'I'm waiting for the verdict. That could take a while.'

'I suppose you expect me to wait for you?'

He was silent for a moment. Then he said, 'Suit yourself.'

'I don't like it when you get sarcastic.' Biddy began to walk slowly back towards Dun Laoghaire.

Anthony followed her. 'Of course I want you to wait for me, Biddy.' He put his arms around her. 'I'm crazy about you.'

'Why didn't you say so in the first place?'

'Because it's only just occurred to me.'

6

The long black car came slowly up the road, its chrome bonnet glittering in the morning sunshine. It stopped outside Santa Maria. The driver climbed out and opened the passenger door, unaware of the curious women who were peeping from behind the curtains.

A tall woman dressed in black and wearing a straw hat stepped out. She swept past the driver and up the steps to the front door, while he took a chamois leather from his pocket and removed the dust that filmed the shiny surface of the car. Mrs Keogh answered the door, and was amazed when the elegant stranger asked to see Mrs Gertrude Doyle.

'Yes.' Mrs Keogh found herself almost curtsying, then standing back to usher her in from the prying eyes of the neighbours.

In the doorway of the sitting-room Mrs Keogh hesitated for an instant, then said, 'Won't you sit down? I'll get Mrs Doyle. What did you say your name was?'

'I didn't.' The mysterious woman smiled, and Mrs Keogh backed out of the room, shutting the door softly.

'There's a very important-looking lady to see you,' Mrs Keogh told Gertie.

'Who is she?' Gertie asked, coming to the top of the stairs in her curious haste.

'I don't know, but she talks like a Yank.'

'Are you sure it was me she said she wanted to speak to?' Gertie asked, removing her overall, and brushing wisps of hair back from her face.

'She said, "Mrs Gertrude Doyle".' Mrs Keogh laughed at Gertie's obvious embarrassment.

The stranger in the sitting-room was smiling when Gertie opened the door. 'Mrs Doyle? Gertie? May I call you Gertie?'

Gertie took the offered hand and said, 'Who might you be?'

'I'm Olive Thornton, Paul's mother.'

'Paul's mother! Why didn't you let me know you were coming? I could have had your room ready. Karen never said anything.'

'I purposely didn't tell Karen because I wanted as little fuss as possible, for Paul's sake. I'm sorry if it's inconvenient.' Her smile was warm.

'Not at all. It's a – great surprise. You must be tired – hungry?'

Olive Thornton waved her hand dismissively. 'I'm fine, really. The journey was quite delightful. I hired a car as soon as I docked in Cobh and drove up slowly.'

'Where are you staying?'

'The Royal Marine Hotel. It was recommended by

Cunard.' The gulf between them narrowed as Gertie sat opposite this gracious lady, whose manner was friendly and direct.

'How is Paul?' Her eyes were anxious.

'He's coming along, considering what's he's been through. There's a doctor from London visiting the Richmond Hospital. The doctors there asked him to see Paul, so he's being kept in for a week or so.'

'I see.'

'The doctor's an expert in that field, and is going to run some more tests on Paul.'

'Yes. Karen wrote me about that doctor. It's fortunate that I'm here to see him.'

'Paul may not recognize you.'

'I know.' Olive Thornton fidgeted with the straps of her bag. 'The thing is, Gertie, I want to see my son, and I'm not waiting any longer. Supposing anything happened to him, and I hadn't seen him?' Her voice was rising.

'I understand, Olive. I'd do exactly the same if it was one of mine.'

'Thank you, Gertie.'

'I think it would be best to alert Karen first, don't you?'

'Oh, of course. Karen has been wonderful. I can't tell you how grateful Paul's father and I are to you and your family.'

'We only did what we could. Anyone would have done the same. Now what about a bite to eat?'

The door opened and John burst in.

'Grandma!'

'John!' Olive threw her arms around him, and hugged him, disregarding her good suit and her fine straw hat, which fell to the floor.

'Easy, John!' Gertie cautioned him.

'I didn't know you were coming. Mom never said.'

'It's a surprise, darling,' Olive gushed. 'Don't you like surprises?'

John nodded. 'Where did you get that car?'

'I hired it. Would you like to ride in it?'

John had pulled back the curtains to reveal a group of children surveying the car, while the chauffeur guarded it jealously with his duster.

Olive laughed. 'You can bring your friends if you like.'

John was indignant. 'They're not my friends.'

Olive replaced her hat, tucking a strand of hair beneath the brim. 'Well, bring whoever you like.'

'Can we call for Patsy?' He looked from one to the other.

'Sure, we'll call for Patsy. Is he your special friend?'

'Patsy's a girl. And she's my best friend.'

'Let's go then.'

John jumped up to go.

'Wait a minute,' Gertie protested. 'I'm not dressed for the Royal Marine. And what about the dinner?'

'Oh, come on, dear,' Olive coaxed. 'I'm sure the hired help can take over for once. Let me talk to your staff.'

Gertie laughed. 'There's only Mrs Keogh, and I don't think she'd appreciate being called the "hired help". She considers herself a part of the family.'

'I'm ready,' John said.

Gertie looked him over. 'Go and wash your hands and face. And change into your new trousers and the jumper I knitted you.'

He had left the room before she had finished talking.

'I'll go and get my hat, if you'll excuse me.'

'Certainly.' Olive smiled. John jumped into the car, disregarding the concerned look on the chauffeur's face. Gertie and Olive followed him.

'My word. Look at this for luxury.' Gertie leant back into the plush interior, and the car drove off, watched by the envious children. The road to Patsy's house was caked with mud and building debris. Women and old people stopped to look as the limousine drew to a halt. The chauffeur stepped out and opened the door for John. Betty Quinn came to the door. 'John, it's you. I thought we had royalty come to visit us.'

'It's my grandmother from America.' John looked solemn-faced and important. 'She's taking us to the Royal Marine for afternoon tea.'

'My word.' Betty called up the stairs, 'Patsy, come quick, John's grandmother from America is here.'

'I'll have to change into my good dress,' Patsy said, when she saw the car.

'Hurry up then.' They motored at a leisurely pace back to Dun Laoghaire, John and Patsy waving to anyone who stopped to stare at them on the way.

Olive Thornton swept past tables covered in white linen,

and laid with fine china, where ladies in flamboyant hats sat nibbling dainty cakes from tiered cake stands. When she found a table large enough for them all to sit at comfortably, she called a waitress.

'This is posh,' Patsy whispered to John, her eyes on the pearl-drop chandelier in the centre of the room.

'Are you hungry?' Olive smiled benevolently at her.

'*I* am, Grandma.' John dragged his eyes from the laden silver trays that the waitresses carried from table to table.

'You haven't changed,' she laughed. 'Do you remember the cookies I used to make for you?'

John nodded. 'And the chocolate brownies.'

Their order for afternoon tea was given, and soon a waitress brought a tray that held sandwiches, cakes, freshly baked scones, and potato cakes.

'How delightful,' Olive gushed. 'Now tuck in children.' She began pouring tea and passing cups around. John ate a triangular sandwich in one mouthful, wiping his buttery fingers on a starched napkin. Patsy, attempting to pick up her cup the way John's grandmother did, extended her little finger as she carried it to her lips. The cup slipped, spilling its contents on to her clean dress.

John burst out laughing.

'Patsy!' Gertie said sharply, jumping up and pulling Patsy up too. 'You've ruined your clean frock.'

Aware of being watched, Patsy was mortified as she gazed down at the sodden mess, and the rivulets of tea running down her legs. Gertie began wiping her dress with a napkin.

'It's the only dress I have.' Patsy's lip trembled.

'Never mind. We'll buy you a new one.' Olive patted her hand. 'Now sit down and enjoy those cakes.'

'Thank you.' Patsy was suddenly overcome with shyness.

'What games do you play together?' Olive asked with exaggerated enthusiasm.

'Hopscotch, skipping, anything,' Patsy replied through a mouthful of cake.

'I like Cowboys and Indians best,' John said. 'Roy Rogers in a film reminds me of America.'

'You'll have to come back for a visit. Would you like that?' Olive asked.

'I'd love it. I'd love to see Grandad again.'

'We're all going over for Lizzie's wedding, please God,' Gertie said. 'She's getting married early next summer in New York.'

'Wonderful. You must be thrilled.'

'I would have preferred to have had the wedding here, but Pete, Lizzie's fiancé, has no family in Ireland, so he's not interested in coming home. Lizzie says it's sensible to have a small wedding there, with the money they'll save on travel.'

'Good idea. You'll have to fork out though.'

'That's why Bill agreed to let me run the guest-house. By the end of the season we should have made a bit of money. If God is good and we keep busy, we'll have a bit extra.'

'Good for you. How is business?'

While Olive and Gertie talked, John and Patsy ate cakes.

Later, in McCullough's draper's, Patsy stared at her unfamiliar reflection in the mirror. The pink satin dress she was trying on made her look much older, and she wasn't sure if her mother would approve of it.

'Don't look so gloomy,' Olive said. 'It's beautiful. Fits you to perfection.'

'Yuk,' John said. 'What a horrible colour.'

'Smile,' Gertie said, 'and try on the blue one.'

Patsy checked the label. 'It costs too much. Mammy would kill me.'

'Nonsense. I'll explain.' Olive ordered the dress with a wave of her hand.

'This is boring,' John said. 'Can we go to the park?'

'Don't be unkind, darling. Have a little patience,' Olive said.

The grey-haired shop assistant smiled at Patsy while Olive paid the bill. 'It suits you,' she said, handing Patsy the bag with her old dress in it.

Karen sat huddled in her chair waiting for their return. Her legs were stiff with the cold, and her knitting lay on her lap untouched. She knew that no matter how sweet Paul's mother was, or how concerned, she was here to take Paul back home to America.

Paul had been so ill. At first he had spent a long time lying in his darkened bedroom, dreaming of hospitals and prisons, often imagining that his room was a prison cell. He was thin and weak, with no desire to escape from the room that enclosed him. Karen had been patient, coaxing. Gradually he began to get a grip on reality. Karen avoided the hubbub of the guest-house, with its constant stream of visitors. Paul found it more restful to keep away from upstairs altogether.

Karen had been strong through her ordeal, but hearing about Olive's visit from Mrs Keogh seemed to undo her. She felt that the pattern of their lives was about to take on a new shape.

When she saw the big black car arrive, and the chauffeur alight, she went upstairs to meet Paul's mother. It was a long time since Karen had seen her, and she expected her to look older, more worn. When Olive came into the hall laughing and exclaiming, her face alive and perfectly made up, Karen was amazed.

'Karen.' She kissed her, then looked at her. 'You look worn out, you poor love. How could it be otherwise.'

Karen said sharply, 'I'm well thank you. I've just got back from the hospital.'

'How is Paul?'

'He's staying in hospital for a few more tests but otherwise he's fine.'

'I can't wait to see him. Now I must get back to the hotel to freshen up, my dear. Come down after supper. We'll have a talk.' She gave Karen's arm a squeeze. 'See you later.'

When John was in bed, Karen went to the Royal Marine and climbed the stairs to Olive's suite. More than anything she wanted to have her wits about her, but she felt confused and tired. A light shone beneath Olive's door, penetrating the corridor. Karen knocked softly.

'Come in.'

Olive was sitting in a comfortable chair in the bay window, looking out at the sea.

'Would you like a drink, my dear?'

'No, thank you, Olive.'

'Tea?'

'Tea would be lovely, thanks.'

Olive rang down to the desk, and ordered tea. The wind outside spattered rain against the windows.

'I was so hopeful for Paul,' she said. 'He was such a bright boy. I suppose I expected too much. You know my happiness was complete when he was born.' She turned to face Karen. 'I'm dying to see my son, Karen. In different circumstances, he would have come home a long time ago.'

'I know, but the fact of the matter is that Paul has been very ill.'

'That's why I want to take him home now. To look after him, care for him.'

'I'm not sure that he's fit to travel yet.'

Olive was not listening.

'I know you've done your best. I'm sorry if I sound unkind.'

The colour flamed in Karen's cheeks.

'I have done everything the doctors advised. And I am a qualified nurse.'

'I know dear. You've done wonders. Now it's time I took over.'

There was a knock on the door. Olive took the tray from the maid. Silently she poured tea, and gave a cup to Karen.

'Paul's father isn't well. He wants to see Paul.' Looking intently at Karen, she added, 'It's my duty to bring him home. You don't honestly think he'll want to stay here forever.'

'I was hoping to bring him for a visit next summer, when we're over for Lizzie's wedding.'

'Anything could happen between now and then.'

'I realize that. But he's being treated here, and he seems happy enough. As happy as he can be.'

'He doesn't seem to be making much progress, and he is entitled to a better life. Imprisonment in a damp basement is hardly conducive to good health.'

Karen stood up. 'I think we had better be careful or we might say things we'll both regret. After all, we both have Paul's interest at heart. He's the one who counts.'

'Quite, my dear. And with Paul's interest at heart, I think it would be better if he came back to the States. He'll get the best medical care there. They have the facilities, and we have the money.'

'His doctors think that it is not a good idea to move him around too much. It confuses him. And there's John to consider. He has had enough upheavals already.'

'Perhaps you would like to stay here. That way you would not have to concern yourself about uprooting John, and you would be saved the unpleasant ordeal of having to see Hank again.' Olive's voice was casual.

In the silence that followed Karen could hear the wind rise. It rattled the window pane. Suddenly she felt removed from the situation, as if what was happening in the room was happening to someone else.

'Believe me, Karen. I have Paul's best interests at heart.' She leaned forward and patted Karen's hand. 'I think he needs a breathing space, and a bit of pampering.'

'What about what I need? Paul is my husband.'

Olive took a cigarette from a packet that lay on the table beside her. She made an elaborate gesture of lighting it before she spoke.

'We have just agreed that it's *Paul's* future that is our main concern. Now if you'll excuse me, I must go to bed. I want to be at the hospital early in the morning, looking my best. We'll talk again tomorrow.'

'I'll see you tomorrow then.'

'Yes dear. I'll call for you at ten o'clock. Meantime don't worry about a thing. I'm here now.'

Karen kissed her on the cheek and left, closing the door softly. She walked slowly along the corridor, as if in a daze, and tiptoed down the dimly lit stairs. A floorboard creaked, and another one, further along, answered with a sigh. The doorman opened the door for her, and she went out into the night.

Her shoes rang hollow on the pavement. A dog barked in the distance, and the wind blew rain into her face. She pulled her coat around her and walked along Windsor Terrace. A light went on in the upstairs window of one of the houses, as an indifferent moon sailed high in a troubled sky.

Dreading the thought of returning home, Karen decided to take the bus to Sallynoggin to see Betty Quinn.

'Karen.' Betty was surprised. 'Come in, you're soaked.'

'I need to talk to someone.'

Betty shuffled into the sitting-room in her slippers. Karen followed.

'I'm sorry to barge in like this.'

'That's all right. I'm glad to see you. Sit down.' Betty threw a log on to the fire. Sparks flew in all directions. 'I'll put the kettle on. No, better still, let's have a drink.' She took a bottle of whiskey and two glasses from the cupboard in the corner and poured a small measure of whiskey into each glass. 'How is Paul?'

'He's all right. His mother's the problem.'

'You weren't expecting her, were you?'

'No. It was a complete surprise.' Karen took a sip of the drink. It made her eyes water. 'He hasn't seen her since he was found in England.'

'A shock.'

'I'm worried about the effect it'll have on him.'

'I don't blame you.'

'She's so anxious to see him that she hasn't given much thought to his health.'

'I suppose you can't blame her for that. Can you imagine if it were John?'

'And she wants to take him back to the States.'

'Mightn't be such a bad idea. You could do with a holiday, not to mention having someone else to look after him for a bit.'

'I was planning on us all going together for Lizzie's wedding. I was really looking forward to it. That's partly why I wanted to go back to work. So I could save up. But she's not prepared to wait that long.'

'Surely Paul's doctors will have a say in it.'

'She'll talk them into letting him go, wait and see. And Mam and Dad will think that she has my best interest at heart, whereas in actual fact I think she wants Paul all to herself.'

'Mothers-in-law! Don't talk to me. They suit themselves if you ask me. That's my experience.' Betty sipped her drink.

'You can say that again.'

'What are you going to do?'

'I really don't know.'

Betty picked up the poker and stoked the fire. Sparks flew up the chimney. 'That's better. Pull your chair nearer if you're cold.'

'I'm warm enough, thanks. I suppose I'm being melodramatic. After all, it isn't the first time Paul has been taken away from me.'

'No. Only this time you can do something about it.'

Karen took a sip of her drink and spluttered. 'God, my stomach's on fire.'

'Won't Paul have something to say about all this?'

'I've no idea. Up until now he hasn't expressed an opinion about anything much.'

'Supposing he goes back with her. What's the worst that can happen to you?'

'I'll manage.'

'That's the spirit.'

'I find it hard going, Betty. Most of the time I pity him. I've so many mixed-up feelings – anger, frustration, disappointment. If only he'd make more of an effort. He doesn't seem to want to.'

'Maybe he can't. Perhaps that's part of his illness. And there's nothing worse than pity. Let him go home with his mother if he wants to. The break will do you both good. And, besides, you can meet up with him in New York. When is she planning on taking him?'

'As soon as he comes out of hospital.'

'You'll feel better once you know what's happening.' Betty poured more whiskey into their glasses and raised hers. 'Here's to Paul and his beloved mother. Tell me about the wedding.'

'Lizzie's thought of everything. She wants to wear Gran's wedding dress.'

'Wouldn't that be a bit faded by now?'

'No, it's in perfect condition. Gran kept it all these years in her trunk, wrapped in brown paper so that no light could yellow the pure white of the material. Mam says she'll take the trunk to New York, with Lizzie's trousseau in it. She's collecting all sorts of bits and pieces for Lizzie's bottom drawer.'

'That'll cost a bob or two.'

'That's why she's slaving away in the guest-house.'

'She looks well though. It suits Gertie to keep occupied, and she needs company.'

'I know. We were worried about her when she lost Gran, and then you lot moved out. The place was like a morgue.'

'She's a marvellous woman. We'd never have got this place only for her, speaking up for us to the council.'

'I didn't know that.'

'She does good turns for everyone. That woman doesn't know the masterpiece of herself.'

Karen laughed, and for a minute they were happy.

'She misses Lizzie terribly. And when Lizzie writes about her life in New York, the walks in the snow through Central Park with Pete, the trips to Long Island in fine weather, the shopping with her friends, the money she's making, Gertie thinks she's never coming back. That thought depresses her.'

'I'm sure it does. But who knows, Lizzie might get tired of that lifestyle someday, especially if she wants to rear a family.'

While Olive and Karen waited in the Outpatients to speak to Paul's doctor, Dr Cole, Olive was hoping that he might cure him. She had no reason to expect miracles. Paul had been seen by many doctors over the past few months. Tests had been done. But their most successful undertaking was the recovery of his speech, and that had been due to hypnosis. They had hoped that under its influence he would also recover his memory, but no matter what method they tried, they were faced with a blank wall. It was as if Paul was refusing to acknowledge the past, and Karen was beginning to accept the fact that it would always be so. As she sat there, leafing through the *Picture Post*, her stomach coiled in a knot of apprehension.

'Mrs Thornton?' A nurse came forward.

'Yes?' they both replied.

'Doctor Cole would like to see you now.'

'I'm his mother. May I see Doctor Cole too?' Olive looked anxiously at the nurse.

'I'll check.' The nurse smiled and left.

When she returned, she confirmed that Doctor Cole would be delighted to see Olive as well, and led the way to the consulting room. Doctor Cole was a distinguished little man, with eyes that twinkled behind his glasses, and a dark moustache.

He shook hands, and invited them to sit down.

'This is a bonus,' he assured Olive. 'I would like to ask you some questions about Paul's past later on, if I may.'

'Certainly, Doctor.' Olive settled herself into her chair.

Doctor Cole consulted the report in front of him, then looked at Karen. 'A typical case of amnesia. I see that good progress has been made with his speech.' His eyes flickered. 'He remembers some things?'

'Yes, doctor. He remembers when we first met, and when our son John was born.'

'I see.' Doctor Cole steepled his hands. 'It's obvious to me that Paul has forgotten what life was like before he became ill. The reason why he wasn't traced before this is because he did not register his address in London. When they discovered him, they were only aware of the fact that he was an American pilot. The tracing agency knew nothing about his marriage, and his home in London, where you lived when you were newly married. I find that strange, don't you?' His eyes looked from one to the other.

'Why didn't he register?' Karen asked.

'Perhaps there wasn't time,' Olive said.

'That is what I have to try to find out. Tell me, Mrs Thornton, how long had you known each other before he went missing?'

'About eighteen months.'

'Was he happy with you?'

'He was never happier. He often told me so.'

'Can you recall any problems he might have had?'

'None.'

'Is he happy now, do you think?'

'I believe he is content.'

Doctor Cole turned to Olive. 'What was his relationship with you and his father like?'

'He adored us. We adored him,' Olive gushed. 'He is an

only child and perhaps he might have felt a little stifled by us at times. Then, of course, becoming a pilot gave him the freedom he craved.'

'So there was a desire to get away, early on, before the war?'

'Yes, doctor.'

'Was he discontented at school?' Doctor Cole searched Olive's face.

Olive frowned resentfully. 'No. He became unhappy when we wanted him to study Forestry, so that he could take over the farm. When he insisted on becoming a pilot, we weren't pleased. You can imagine how we felt when he volunteered to help train British pilots.'

'Quite.' Doctor Cole wrote some notes, then said, 'So he was a determined young man.'

'Determined to fly aeroplanes. He was easy-going about everything else. Especially the farm. He didn't show a great deal of interest in it.'

'I see. Well the fact that he has recovered his speech indicates to me that he still has that determination in him for what he wants – and I stress that. It also makes me believe that there is every chance that he will recover his memory. But we mustn't rush things, or make him feel under any strain.'

'I would like to take him home to the States, doctor,' Olive said.

'When did you have in mind?'

'As soon as he's well enough.'

'As I already said, we mustn't rush things. It would be a

good idea to wait until he's finished his treatment, in about two months, and his doctors here are satisfied that they have done all they can for him.'

'May I see him, doctor?' Olive asked almost meekly.

'Certainly. Only for a few minutes today, and in my presence. I want to see his reaction.'

'Yes, doctor.'

Drowsy from the medication they had given him, Paul lay in bed half asleep, his head to one side. For once his face was clear of anxiety.

'Paul?' Olive's face was white as she called her son's name.

He turned his head. A look of enquiry crossed his face, and it was obvious to Karen that he did not recognise his mother.

'Paul, I'm your mother.' Olive's voice was quavering. Suddenly recognition suffused his face, and as her arms embraced him, the bafflement in his expression was replaced by joy.

Two weeks later Olive left for the States, alone. Paul, Karen and John accompanied her to the airport. It was a cold, blustery day with winds threatening to rise to gale force. Shivering and with a protective arm around Paul, Olive suggested tea in the Shamrock Lounge, while she waited to board the aircraft. John's excitement at watching a small plane descend from the sky amused Paul at first, but as it came closer to the runway he suddenly jumped up and began shouting, 'It's going to crash! Watch out, it's going to crash!'

'What's the matter?' Ashen-faced, Olive tried to restrain him, but he would not listen, or budge from the window.

'I've flown one like that,' he shouted, 'and it crashed. They're dangerous machines. You've got to keep out of the way.'

'Paul, you remember. Olive, he remembers.' Karen suddenly burst into tears and tried to move close to him, but his flailing arms prevented her.

'Remember what? Why are you crying?' Paul looked at her in astonishment.

'That you flew an aeroplane. And crashed it.' Paul sat down, and put his head in his hands. His whole body was shaking. People seated at nearby tables looked both alarmed and embarrassed.

'Yes,' he said. 'I remember. I remember that my parachute wouldn't open at first, and I thought I was done for. I landed in a wooded area – how I missed the trees I don't know. And I hurt my leg. I couldn't walk properly for ages.' Suddenly he looked up. 'It was in France.' The story was pouring out in a jumble of words.

'Oh my poor darling,' Olive said. 'How awful for you.'

'But he remembers,' Karen kept saying through her tears.

John was chanting, 'He remembers, he remembers.'

By the time Olive's flight was called, Paul had recounted the details of his capture and detention in a German jail.

Olive, loath to say good-bye, hugged and kissed him repeatedly.

'You will come home as soon as the doctors allow you to? Now write and tell me everything, Karen. Be sure and tell Doctor Cole exactly what happened here today. In fact, I'll write to him myself.'

'Don't fuss, Mom,' Paul said. 'We'll see you at Lizzie's wedding in June if not beforehand.'

Paul held his mother close for a few moments, then with a final hug to each of them, she was gone through the barriers.

From the balcony of the airport they watched her walk out to the plane. When she reached the top of the steps she turned, blew them kisses, and waved.

As the plane took off, an east wind whipped against their legs. Karen pulled her coat around her and took Paul's arm. 'Come on, darling. We'd better go. I can't wait to get home to tell them the news.'

Paul looked perplexed. 'And to think that all this was locked inside me.'

'There's a lot more to come out, darling. Let's try and take it in easy stages, so that you won't get too exhausted.'

Chatting and holding hands tightly, they made their way to the carpark, desperate to tell Gertie and Bill the news.

7

Anthony was in the sitting-room listening to the radio when he heard the front door open. He knew it was his father. Bob Quinn appeared in the doorway.

'So this is what it means to be out of work. Well for some.'

'You're early.' Anthony got up, crossed the room, and turned off the radio.

'I came home specially to see you before you went off on one of your escapades again.'

Betty came into the room. 'Cup of tea?'

'No.'

'I'll make one anyway.' She returned to the kitchen. They could hear her putting the kettle on.

'Do you think it's convenient for us to have a chat?' Anthony's father asked. Anthony clenched his fists to quell the fury his father's sarcasm always triggered in him.

'I'm all ears.' He saw a flicker of the reaction his own brand of sarcasm set off in his father's eyes.

'Good.' Bob Quinn sat down, and made himself comfortable. 'I'm worried about you.'

'There's no need.' Anthony had returned to his seat, but sat on the edge of it.

'You don't seem to be getting very far.'

'Very far where?'

'Nowhere. That's what I mean. What are you going to do with your life?'

'It's *my* life.'

'Oh, very smart. But it's me that's keeping you. When did you last earn a decent few shillings?'

Betty returned and handed Bob a cup of tea. She hovered in the doorway, as if anticipating trouble.

'You're not paying bed and board here,' Bob said.

'I didn't know it was a problem.'

'It isn't, son,' his mother said, but his father continued as if she had not spoken.

'So we keep you, while you sit around and drink and sleep half the day or most of the day, and then go off gallivanting all night.'

'Bob.' Betty put her hand to her forehead, as if to quell the pain there.

'What?'

'Anthony's down on his luck at the moment.'

'That moment happened a while ago now. How long is he going to be mooning around for? That's what I want to know. If he doesn't do something useful with his life now, he'll come to a bad end.'

'What did you have in mind?' Anthony asked politely.

'Something like a job, son, or an apprenticeship. You'll be

trained for nothing if you don't get a move on.'

'I'll get a job.'

'Where, may I ask? They're few and far between.'

'I wasn't thinking of here. There's nothing to keep me here anyway.'

'Oh, I see. Did you hear that, Betty? That'll show you the consideration he gives his parents.'

'Stop that, Bob.'

'Where will you get a job?' Bob asked. Anthony was frowning as he gazed earnestly out of the window, concentrating on the piles of bricks on the opposite side of the road. There was silence. Bob moved restlessly in his chair. Betty darted glances from one to the other.

Finally Bob said, 'It's your life, son, I'll grant you that. But you realize the consequences, don't you?'

'What consequences?'

'Being a good-for-nothing all your life. What about Mr Healy and your apprenticeship?'

'I left Mr Healy behind a long time ago, and I've no intention of going back.'

'And why haven't you, if it's not too rude a question?'

'Because carpentry is not the life for me.'

'Too high and mighty for you.'

'No. It's not interesting enough.'

'And loafing around is?'

'It's not Anthony's fault.' Betty moved into the room, interposing herself between them. 'Look what happened with the boxing. Now if that wasn't bad luck . . .'

'And I suppose you're going to tell me that he had nothing to do with that?'

'You think it was all my fault?'

'I didn't say that. What I am saying is that you can't sit around mooning over what might have been, or waiting for an opportunity to fall into your lap. You have to get out and do something about it.'

'I'll make my own decisions about my future – when I'm good and ready.' Anthony was angry.

'And that's your final word?' His father stood up, suddenly looking tired.

'Yes, that's my final word.'

'Well if that's your attitude, I'd like you to leave this house. Take some responsibility on your own shoulders for a change.'

'Bob.' Betty looked aghast.

'It's all right, Mam,' Anthony said. 'I'll be glad to go.'

'That way you'll have to get a job,' Bob continued as if Anthony had not spoken.

'I have an offer of a job. But I was waiting to hear from Mr Murphy.'

Betty said, 'You won't hear until that poor fellow you knocked out is well again, and that could take a long time.'

'Where is this job?' Bob asked.

'Belfast.'

'How did you hear about it?'

'Pal of mine in London.'

'Doing what?'

'Labouring on a building site.'

'Take it,' Bob said, and left.

'I'm still hoping to be able to continue with the boxing,' Anthony said when he had gone. 'Anyway, I wouldn't admit it to his face, but the oul fella's right. It's time I took charge of my own life.'

'It'll make you realize the cost of living.'

'Spud might give me something temporary, while I'm waiting.'

A few days later Anthony got a temporary job in Connolly's Grocery Shop, in Patrick Street, to earn some money for the fare and accommodation in Belfast. It was a cut price shop. Tom Connolly was waging a solitary price war on big grocery stores like Findlater's and Lipton's, and business was booming. Extracts from the newspapers were pasted in the window confirming Mr Connolly's heroic battle, and prices were compared and slashed in huge red letters over every item in the window.

Anthony worked late packing groceries in cardboard boxes, and delivering them well into the evening. Then the floor was swept, and the shop tidied. He liked the brown overall he wore, and the particular spicy smell of the shop.

After work he would stay in Dun Laoghaire, wandering around, or chatting to Spud or Rasher, who owned a bicycle repair shop off York Road. Anthony often talked to customers — anyone who was free for a chat, and anything to prolong the business of going home. He felt removed from the price war, and the excitement it generated among the women of Dun Laoghaire. He was more of a spectator than a performer, and that feeling saved him the trouble of thinking too much about anything.

Spud and he drove around late at night in Spud's father's car. Sometimes they went to a dance in the Top Hat Ballroom, mainly to listen to the band. Occasionally there was a party in someone's house. One Saturday Janet Shaw held a party. Biddy was there, talking to a fellow Anthony had never seen before. She was wearing make-up and her hair was loose around her shoulders, making her look older. As she talked her face became animated, and when she laughed, Anthony grew jealous. He wanted to share the joke, or break the other fellow's neck for engaging Biddy's undivided attention. Later he met her in the hall.

'Do you want a lift home with us?' he asked.

'That'd be great. Thanks.'

'That was a great party,' Biddy said as they drove off. 'It's nice to get away from the same kind of people all the time.'

'Yeh,' Anthony said. 'I noticed that you were enjoying yourself. You like hob-nobbing with Janet's snotty friends, don't you?'

'Yes. I like a bit of class.'

'I didn't notice you objecting to them,' Spud said to Anthony.

'It was all right. Somewhere to go.'

'When are you going away?' Biddy asked.

'Soon I expect. The oul fella has given me my marching orders.'

'You'll never come back.'

Anthony took out his cigarettes, lit one and inhaled deeply. 'What makes you say that?'

'Because I know lots of people who went away with every intention of coming back. They never did.'

'I suppose it all depends on whether I've a future as a boxer or not.'

'When will you know?'

'Soon I hope. The waiting's killing me.'

'Why don't you go to the Tech? Learn something.'

'Takes too long. Anyway I'm tired of all that. I hated school. Never learnt anything there. Couldn't wait to get out.'

'I'd love to design clothes . . . you know, become a fashion designer.'

Anthony whistled. 'Tall order. You're good at drawing though, I'll grant you that.'

'I could design my own clothes.'

Anthony's thoughts were miles away. 'I don't think I can stay at home much longer,' he said. 'The oul fella's very jittery; can't wait to see the back of me.' He blew out cigarette smoke.

'It can't be that bad. Not as bad as it is for me.'

'Is it?' Anthony looked at her.

She pulled a face. 'All I want is an education. That seems to make me some kind of monster in my mother's eyes.'

'She's got a hard life, Biddy. She's doesn't mean you any harm.'

He was remembering all the things he had wanted to do for Biddy, and all the things he had wanted to show her. It occurred to him that the responsibility her mother had placed upon her had matured her. He saw too, for the first time, that that same responsibility had made her lonely. A feeling of tenderness for her swept over him. Suddenly he wanted to protect and help her. He reached over and put his arm around her. She rested her head on his shoulder. For a moment there was silence. Then Spud drew to a halt outside her house and said, 'We're here, folks.'

Anthony got out and walked Biddy to her front door. He stood there awkwardly as she turned the key carefully in the lock.

'Would you like to come to the pictures in Dublin next week? Before I take off.'

'I don't think you're ever going away.'

'I'll be going all right. Anyway, will you come?'

'That'd be nice. We're very busy in the guest-house though.'

'Can you get Friday evening off?'

'I'll ask Mrs Doyle.'

'Great.'

'I'd better go in before me mother wakes up.'

He looked at her in the dark and felt that she was already out of his reach.

8

Biddy took the train to Dublin, and sat in the carriage beside a woman with a baby in her arms. She smiled at the baby. The train chugged out of the station and steam rose and evaporated as they approached the West Pier. Fishing boats quietly nudged one another in the harbour. As the train gathered speed, Biddy sat back and began to relax. She felt excited and grown-up at the idea of having a date in Dublin city.

The train rattled on, and began to sway from side to side. It flew past the marsh in Booterstown, where flocks of birds were gathered. Soon the fields ran into houses, neatly dissected by narrow back gardens. Then the gardens disappeared, to be replaced by backyards. At last the train steamed into the city, past office buildings where people sat at desks in dimly lit windows. Anthony was standing on the platform, his eyes searching the carriages. Biddy ran to meet him.

'Hello, Biddy.'

'Howaya.'

With his arm around her, he walked her down the

steps and into the busy streets. 'You look great.'

'Thanks.' Biddy blushed.

'I thought we'd have something to eat first.'

'Good. I'm starving.'

The cold air hit them as they turned towards Butt Bridge. Anthony tightened his arm around her waist.

Biddy smiled up at him. 'I got a new dress.'

He gave her a hug.

'What have you been doing?'

'This and that.'

He kept his face averted, watching the traffic, and guided her across the street as soon as a policeman, who was directing traffic in the centre aisle, gave the signal. Cars, buses, horses and carts waited impatiently on either side of them. They walked in silence until they came to the Metropole. The foyer was warm, and there was a delicious smell of cooking. Anthony led her upstairs to the restaurant. Chrome trays of chips, sausages, rashers and beans sat snugly in hot plates. Biddy's mouth watered.

'What'll you have?'

'A bit of everything.'

Anthony laughed. 'Get us a table. I'll bring the food.'

She found a table in a corner and watched the enormous silver tea-urn in front of Anthony emitting wisps of smoke, as water churned inside it. Finally he returned, carrying a tray with two steaming plates of food. Placing one plate in front of her, he sat down.

'We haven't got too much time. The main feature starts at eight.'

'I can't eat as fast as you.' She was watching him stuff a forkful of chips into his mouth.

'I'm starving.'

She ate a few mouthfuls. 'What exactly will you be working at?'

He tapped his nose with his finger and said, 'Eat up.'

Biddy put down her knife and fork. 'Do you know something?'

'What?'

'You're a pain in the neck.'

They continued eating in silence. After a while Anthony said, 'I don't know exactly what I'll be doing, Biddy. I'll let you know. Would you like some dessert when you're finished? They've got your favourite chocolate sundae.'

'Do we have time?'

He checked his watch. 'Just about — if you stop talking. You can have two chocolate sundaes if you stop asking questions.'

'One will be enough, thank you.'

Anthony joined the queue.

The dining-room began to fill up. Dishes clattered in the kitchen, and voices rose and fell as people smiled and talked to one another.

Anthony returned. The chocolate sauce on Biddy's sundae glistened.

'What's on your mind?' Anthony said.

Biddy shrugged. 'I was wondering how they make the chocolate. It's nice and soft.'

'Divine.' Anthony leaned over and took her hand. 'Like you.'

'I'm going away myself next week.'

'Why didn't you tell me?'

'I only heard yesterday.'

'Where?'

'County Waterford. I've got a job looking after a little boy of three there.'

'Where will you stay?'

'I'll live in.'

'Will you write to me?'

'How can I when you won't give me your address?'

'I'll give you an address when I have a proper one. And don't give it to anyone else.'

'I won't.'

'I'll write back and I'll tell you all about Belfast and the job.'

'Great.' They finished their meal and went into the cinema.

When Biddy saw the tall elaborate gates, and the sweeping drive up to the big white house, she assumed that her new employers, Commander and Mrs Price, would be snobs.

A woman with drooping shoulders and a long check apron answered the door.

'Hello. I'm Biddy Plunkett. I've come to work here,' Biddy said.

'Thought you might be.' The woman lowered her voice. 'Her Ladyship is waiting for you in the dining-room. I'll take you to her.'

'Thanks.'

'I'm Molly, the housekeeper.'

Molly took her through a highly polished hall, panelled in dark wood. Ancient portraits hung on the walls. She patted the bun at the nape of her neck, and straightened her apron outside one of the closed doors, before knocking.

'Don't be nervous. She's not as frightening as she looks.'

Biddy nodded.

A voice called, 'Come in.'

Mrs Price was sitting at the head of a beautifully laid table, wearing a heavily embroidered satin gown. Her hair was brushed high on her head and was held with a large gold clasp. In a deferential manner Molly leaned towards her. 'This is Biddy, the new girl, ma'am.'

Big dark eyes gazed at her and for a second Biddy had a bewildering sense of having walked on to another planet. Then Mrs Price spoke. 'I am aware of that, Molly.' She smiled at Biddy. 'Come and have something to eat before Thomas wakes up from his nap.' She indicated a chair. Molly left, closing the door quietly behind her.

'It's very kind of you to go to this trouble for me.' Biddy looked admiringly at the white cloth on the table, the plate of thin cut bread and butter, the cucumber sandwiches, cakes and biscuits, and bowls of different kinds of jam.

Monica Price laughed dismissively. 'Molly prepared it. Now tuck in, you must be hungry.'

Biddy helped herself to a slice of thin bread and butter and heaped strawberry jam on it.

'Milk?' Monica Price asked when she had poured her tea.

'Yes, please.'

A man appeared in the doorway. Tall, with receding hair, he gazed at Biddy intensely. Finally he said, 'You must be Biddy. I'm Commander Price.'

'Yes, sir,' was all Biddy could think to say, suddenly conscious that her dress was shabby and a size too small.

'Let's hope you won't find it too quiet here. I know young girls like to be with their friends.' He took his place at the other end of the table.

'Don't put her off, darling,' Monica Price admonished.

'On the contrary, Molly will be glad of the company. It can be quite dull here.' There was an air of gravity in the smile he gave Biddy.

Biddy found herself straightening her back, and lifting her cup up to her lips.

'I hardly hired the girl for Molly's amusement, dear.' Monica Price glared at him, and turning to Biddy said, 'Life's never dull with Thomas around. And my husband is rarely here. He's off again tomorrow; back to his ship.'

Commander Price said, 'Duty calls.'

They ate in silence for a while. Biddy, reaching for a

cucumber sandwich, was afraid to speak in case she might say something stupid.

Eventually Monica Price folded her napkin, and rose from the table. 'When you're finished I'll show you around before Thomas wakes up.'

Biddy blessed herself and followed her, eager to see the rest of the house. The upstairs rooms were large and airy. Thomas's room, the smallest in the house, was next to Biddy's. Monica opened the door quietly and went in.

'There you are, darling. This is Biddy. She's come to take you for a walk.' She gave the three-year-old boy a kiss on the cheek as she lifted him out of his cot.

He gazed at Biddy, his cheeks red, his little mouth creasing into a smile.

'Hello.' Biddy took his hand, but he pulled it away, and pointing a chubby finger at the window said, 'Boat, boat.'

'Yes, darling. Biddy will take you down to see the boat. Let's get you ready.'

Biddy and Thomas, wrapped up warmly against the east wind, went down to the beach. It smelt of dried seaweed. Thomas ran along the water's edge, with Biddy chasing him. A boat, half out of the water, lay with its hull on the pebbly sand. It was moored to an iron ring that was welded to a rock. Gulls flew in and out of it and perched on its prow. Biddy lifted Thomas and swung him into the boat. The gulls screeched away in disgust. Thomas laughed with delight as the boat rocked. Waves slapped against its side, and sprayed him.

'Let's go. The tide's coming in,' Biddy called. Thomas refused to budge. He wriggled in protest as Biddy hauled him out. 'I'll bring you back tomorrow,' she promised, kissing the top of his silky head.

It was difficult to get to know anyone apart from Monica and Thomas. Biddy missed home. Monica seemed to insinuate herself into every available space of Biddy's life, so that she had no time for herself. Thomas liked her. She gathered shells for him and showed him different coloured stones, teaching him how to count by placing them in a row and pointing out: one, two, three. When she took him into the water, she held his hand, never taking her eyes off him. Thomas loved the texture of wet sand, and the destruction his tiny fingers and feet wrought on Biddy's carefully crafted sand castles. Monica Price had strict rules about bringing up Thomas which she applied rigidly. 'Children should be seen and not heard' was her motto. When Thomas went to crawl up on to her lap she would say, 'Don't hang on to me. Go and play with your toys,' and push him off the arm of the sofa. He would cry, and Biddy would pick him up. She would take him by the hand to bathe him, or read him stories. Monica would call out to her to leave him on his own for a little while. 'He'll never be a man if he's mollycoddled,' she would say.

While Thomas slept, Biddy helped Molly make beds and prepare vegetables for the elaborate evening meals. Molly, an ageing woman from the outskirts of the town, gave Biddy a comforting feeling. Sometimes Biddy picked flowers from the garden and arranged them in huge vases to brighten up the house. She wrote home often, telling Annie and May all about Thomas and his quirky ways, and assuring her mother that she was well and happy. Annie and May wrote her long letters in return. The scrawly writing begged her to hurry up and come home. Her mother would add a few brief words at the bottom of the page, reminding Biddy of how busy she was.

Monica Price occasionally found fault with Biddy's work. She would single out something small that Biddy was unaware of, like a crease in the front of a shirt she had ironed. Biddy would try to do better next time, knowing that what Monica said was for her own good. Biddy was grateful to her for giving her the freedom to have a life away from Dun Laoghaire, her family, and Anthony. She happily pushed Thomas for miles in his pram, singing to him and collecting leaves on the way to dip in glycerine and preserve, or wild flowers to arrange on Monica's dressing-table.

They went for picnics in the woods, and walks along the beach, that ended when Thomas would stand resolutely in front of the boat shouting, 'Boat, boat', to Biddy. Sometimes, on their return, Biddy would hear snippets of news on the radio about the military activity in the North, or men arrested at the Border. She would wonder about Anthony – where he was, what he was doing.

'Penny for your thoughts,' Molly said one day, when she saw the preoccupied expression on Biddy's face.

'Hardly worth it.'

Molly placed a bowl of potatoes down in front of her. 'The idle grow weary. Peel the spuds.'

'I'm worried about Anthony.'

'Why? Where is he?'

'I'm not sure. That's the trouble.'

'Don't let him get the better of you. You have plenty to look forward to.'

Biddy was thinking of the thud her heart made when he kissed the side of her neck, his head warm and nestling into hers.

Biddy was sitting on a high-backed chair, shelling peas and occasionally popping them in her mouth, when there was a knock on the back door. Monica Price was out shopping and Molly had a day off. She answered it, thinking it was the bread man.

Anthony stood there.

'What are you doing here?'

'Thought I'd surprise you. Coming for a spin?' He indicated the gleaming motor bike parked outside the gate.

'That yours?' Biddy gazed at it in amazement.

'No. I robbed it on my way here. Aren't you going to ask me in?'

'Sorry,' Biddy stood back to let him pass. 'Will you have a cup of tea?' Biddy reached for the kettle before he had time to answer.

'That'd be nice.' He took his cigarettes from his pocket, and lit one.

'I thought you'd given them up.'

'I had.'

'Didn't last long.'

Anthony inhaled deeply. 'Can you get the evening off?'

'I don't know.' Biddy looked doubtful.

'I'll ask if you like.'

'Great.'

The kitchen was warm and Anthony sat down at the table.

'How long have you got?' Biddy looked at the clock.

'Today.'

'That's not long. You're always on the move. What's Belfast like?'

'Not bad.'

'Do you like the job?'

'It's work. That's the best I can say about it.'

They were silent while they drank their tea. Biddy eventually said, 'You've lost weight.'

Anthony flexed his muscles. 'Doing a bit of training. That won't do me any harm. Sugar Ray Robinson won the world middleweight boxing title. He beat Jake LaMotta in Chicago.'

'So?'

'So now Randy Turpin wants to take on Robinson in London. He used to be a Merchant Navy cook. If he can take on someone like Sugar Ray, then there's hope for the likes of me.'

'That's if they let you back into the game. Have you heard from Mr Murphy?'

'Any day now. If they let me back, I'm giving up this job and going.'

'Good for you. That'd be great, Anthony. You might come up against Sugar Ray Robinson some day.'

Anthony laughed. 'Randy Turpin would do me fine.'

They heard the key in the front door. Biddy went into the hall.

'My friend Anthony is here,' she said to Monica Price. 'I wasn't expecting him.'

'Hello, Mrs Price.' Anthony came to meet her. 'I'm Anthony Quinn; pleased to make your acquaintance.'

Monica shook hands with him.

'Biddy told me all about you.'

'Nothing too drastic, I hope.' Anthony smiled.

Monica Price preened herself. 'Nothing but the best.' She winked at Biddy and turned to take off her coat.

'I hope Biddy offered you a cup of tea.'

'Yes thanks. I was admiring your home. Biddy is lucky to be here.'

'You're very kind.'

'I was hoping to take her out to the country for a spin on my bike.'

'Of course. Take her to Tramore. Treat her to her tea. I'll manage Thomas myself. Take these parcels up to my room, Biddy, and get yourself ready.'

'Are you sure?'

'Run along before I change my mind.'

'Thanks.' Biddy flew up to her room.

'You're an angel, Mrs Price.' Anthony meant it. 'I'm very grateful.'

'Not at all, Anthony. Now tell me all about yourself while you're waiting.'

Anthony showed Biddy how to sit on the pillion.

'The trick is to hold on tight.' He placed his goggles over his eyes.

The bike roared to life and they rode off, Anthony expertly negotiating the twists and turns of the road.

Biddy locked her arms around his waist, and let her hair stream back in the wind. When they reached Tramore, Anthony slowed down and cut the engine.

'Would you like to have some tea?' he asked. 'And a rest?'

Biddy slipped off the bike and straightened herself. 'Look at the state of me.'

He watched as she straightened her skirt, and smoothed down her hair. 'You look lovely,' he said.

The streets were quiet in the afternoon, with only a few people out walking. An old man stood in a doorway smoking a pipe, a cat curled at his feet. They walked on towards the beach. It was deserted. The wind swept over the swollen waves, making patterns on them. Anthony looked up at the sky. 'It's trying to rain.'

Biddy shivered and pulled her coat around her. 'That'll make a change,' she said with mock sarcasm.

'Not much of a day for a walk on the beach.'

'I'm glad you came.'

'I wasn't sure how I'd manage it. I thought I might have to bring Spud with me.'

'I wouldn't have minded.' They stopped and looked at one another.

Biddy said, 'Are you going back to Dun Laoghaire tonight?'

''Fraid so. Belfast tomorrow.'

'You don't seem very enthusiastic about your job.'

'How could you be enthusiastic about labouring?'

'Why don't you come home?'

Anthony shrugged. 'Soon. Let's sit down for a bit.'

They found a flat rock among a group of rocks that jutted out from the sea, and sat close together.

'Do you like it here?' Anthony asked.

'It's all right. Mrs Price is good to me. I love Thomas.'

Anthony took his cigarettes and matches out of his pocket, and cupped his hands to light one.

'How's your friend Seán?'

'He spends most of his time in London.'

'You're not telling me much. I feel I don't know you any more – if I ever did.' Her voice died on the wind as she threw out her hands in a helpless gesture.

'It's nobody's business what I do. I come and go as I please,' Anthony shouted at her.

'It is my business what you do, Anthony,' Biddy said quietly.

'No it isn't.'

'Then why did you bother coming to see me?'

'I told you already. I missed you.'

She shivered. 'I hope you're not in some kind of trouble.'

'You really do let your imagination run away with you, Biddy.' His face was indignant.

The wind whipped up around them and he caught her. She stood rigid against him. He pressed his face close to hers. Hers was cold.

'Everything's all right. Stop worrying about me.' Not for the first time Biddy wished she had a wide range of words to express herself more eloquently.

'I think of the past. All the hopes we had.' She was talking more to herself than to him.

'Go on, say what you have to say. I want to hear it.'

'It's like all these forces are pulling against each other all the time.'

'I don't understand.'

After a pause she said, 'I think of you all the time. But there's this . . . tension between us. I want everything to be nice.'

Anthony's voice was shaky when he spoke. 'You want everything to be nice. Well, life's not like that. And if you think that, then you have a lot of growing up to do, Biddy Plunkett.'

She burst into tears.

'Biddy, I'm sorry.' The words were whispered softly as he

took her in his arms and for a second Biddy wondered if he had said them.

They stood holding each other as the rain began to move in squalls across the road.

'It's lashing,' Biddy said. 'Let's shelter somewhere.'

They ran and hid beneath the branches of a big tree.

Later, Biddy let herself in through the front door. The house was in darkness, apart from the dim light on the landing. There was a plate of sandwiches, covered with a serviette, and a small bottle of lemonade on the kitchen table. She sat down and began to eat slowly. Everything was quiet, warm and familiar, and she was happy to let herself drift into the temporary feeling of safety the house gave her.

Tomorrow would be another uneventful day. Thomas would come bouncing into her room, shouting for her to wake up. She would dress him, feed him, take him for a walk, and do all the things she always did. He would not know there was anything different about her. But Biddy would. Already she knew that after tonight she would never be the same person again.

When her plate and glass were washed, she put out the light. The moon shone into the window of her bedroom, casting its faint light on the bed-head. The same moon that shone on Anthony who was, at this moment, on his way back to Dun Laoghaire and Belfast. Suddenly she felt the desolation of being separated from him.

9

It was Christmas Eve. Patsy had permission to do her Christmas shopping with John, and attend midnight Mass with the Doyle family. She had bought lavender soap for her mother, Brylcreem for her father, a comb for Anthony, and a sixpenny bar of Cadbury's Dairy Milk each for Damien and Brian. The rest of her money had gone to buy John a Dinky car.

As they queued up to purchase red crepe wrapping paper and ribbon, there was a feeling of impatience around them. The shop assistant cut the ribbon off a large spool, and John, with an air of resignation, said to Patsy, 'She can't wait to see the back of us.'

Patsy shrugged. 'Our money is as good as anyone else's.'

Once out in bustling George's Street, they hunched in their coats, and walked on. The shops were decorated with holly and fairy lights, and sometimes a crib. In the baker's they bought a dozen iced buns – a treat for Gertie, who considered shop cakes to be an extravagance. The Monument Creamery had blocks of golden butter, globes of cheeses, and large brown eggs resting in baskets of straw.

Patsy bought the butter and eggs that Gertie ordered, and had enough money left to buy a slab of Cleeve's toffee for John's Christmas stocking.

'Is that all?' the shop assistant asked as she wrapped the butter in greaseproof paper.

'Yes, thank you,' Patsy said, too pleased with her purchases to notice the scolding tone.

The night was clear, but the cold burned John's ears. On their way to the bus stop they passed weary shoppers trudging home, their shopping bags weighing them down. At the park they waited for the bus. It was dark and silent, in contrast to the well-lit, busy shops. An old man shuffled along, scuffing the pavement with his worn shoes. Patsy called out 'Happy Christmas' to him. He saluted her and passed on. When they got back to Santa Maria there was nobody in.

'Where is everybody?' Patsy asked.

'I dunno. Come and see the Christmas tree,' John said.

John brought her up to the sitting-room, and plugged in the lights on the tree. The walls reflected their colours in tiny rainbows. Carefully wrapped presents were piled underneath, and Patsy sat on the floor to read out the names on the cards attached to them.

'I wonder where they went?' Patsy fingered the parcels that seemed to her at that minute to be the cohesion of the whole family.

John went down to the kitchen. There was a note on the

table. 'Gone to visit Mrs Troy with Gertie. See you in the church at 9 pm, Mom.'

Just as he finished reading the message he heard Bill's car shuddering to a halt outside. Bill came up the front steps, and put his key in the lock as John opened the door.

'Patsy's here,' John said. 'She's coming to midnight Mass with us. Mom left a note to meet her in the church at nine o'clock. Is that not too early?'

'No. There's the procession to the crib, and we'll want to get a place.'

The car was cold. Bill gave Patsy a rug to wrap around her legs as they drove through the deserted streets. Patsy and John counted Christmas trees in windows as they passed. As they approached the church, they could hear singing and Patsy could feel the excitement of Christmas mounting inside her. The church was crowded. People stood, blocking the view of the altar, their voices raised in joyful harmony as they sang 'Silent Night'. The children followed Bill up the aisle, searching for Gertie and Karen on their way.

John saw them. Gertie's head was turned, watching for the priest to approach with the baby Jesus. It reminded him of the times she would take him to Mass, and wait with patience for the priest to come out on to the altar. She would watch in rapt attention as the Mass began, her face a concentration of prayer. John knew that the Mass, and the priest's sermon after the gospel, lifted Gertie out of her humdrum existence and gave her hope.

Now, standing beside her, John felt her joy as she gazed at the altar, banked with red and white carnations, green holly leaves entwined among them.

The choir sang and the congregation rose to join in. Karen nudged John to sing. Patsy sang too, coughing and spluttering until her throat ached. She felt too hot in her red woollen dress.

The boom of the organ made her head spin, and suddenly everything was spinning: the altar, the statues, the angels carved into the high pillars. Before she knew what was happening, she was outside, sitting on a bench in the porch, Gertie's arms around her. People stopped on their way out of the church to see how she was. John, eyes downcast and anxious about Patsy, waited silently while Bill went to get the car.

Gertie put her to bed, and the doctor came and examined her.

'Open your mouth, and let me have a look at your throat. Good girl.' He sat on the side on the bed. 'You have a touch of fever. Best keep you in bed for a few days.'

'Over Christmas?'

'I'm sorry.' He heaved his shoulders in a gesture of helplessness, and then said quietly to Gertie. 'It's tonsillitis, but because of her history we'd better be cautious.'

'Will she have to go to hospital?'

'Not unless she gets worse. Tell her mother to keep her in bed, and keep the room at an even temperature.'

Patsy was dreaming about Christmas. When she opened her eyes, she saw John standing there.

'Are you feeling better?' he asked.

'You shouldn't be here,' Patsy croaked, every word hurting her.

He sat on the bed and took her hand. 'I don't care. I couldn't stand it if you were to get sick again.'

Patsy blushed and gazed into the distance. 'Don't be silly,' she managed to say.

When he had gone, Patsy cried, but not because of the fear of a recurrence of the TB that had nearly killed her. She was thinking of the roller-skates she was hoping to get for Christmas, and that she might be too weak to use for a long time.

The next morning Bill wrapped a warm rug around her and carried her down to the car. John sat in the back seat with her. Betty put her to bed and assured Bill that she would keep her there until her temperature was back to normal.

When they returned, the tree was on, its lights winking through the room's tall window. John ran up the steps and hurled himself into the room as soon as Bill opened the hall door. He crouched down to get his presents out from under the tree and Bill knelt down with him. As he straightened up, John noticed how Bill's hairline had receded considerably, and that his face was more creased than before.

'Look at all these.' Bill spread out his hands to gather all the presents with John's name on them.

John grabbed the biggest parcel and unwrapped it.

'A train set from Santa!'

As they began to fit the parts together, Karen came into the room, followed by Gertie carrying a tray of drinks. They sat by the fire, watching as Bill set out the tracks, and assembled the carriages. Gertie sipped her sherry, then set it down carefully on the table beside her.

'Have you heard from Olive recently?' Gertie said quietly.

Karen leaned forward, her eyes luminous in the firelight. 'Yes. She wants us to go out there as soon as Paul is well enough.'

There was silence. Gertie rested her elbow on the fat upholstered armchair, and gazed into the fire. Then she said, 'You know you have our support, whatever you decide.'

After a pause Karen said, 'I think we'll go back for the wedding, and stay for a while.'

Gertie watched her steadily. 'Olive would want her grandson to be an American eventually.'

Karen watched the flames lick the side of the black grate.

Gertie continued. 'She would say that there are more opportunities for John out there.'

'They have a magnificent place,' Karen said. 'Plenty of space, horses, freedom, everything money can buy, and Hank's desperate to get his greedy hands on it.'

'That's another consideration. A big one if you ask me. After all, it is John's inheritance.'

'There's something else that has to be taken into account.' Karen looked at her mother.

'What?'

'I think I'm pregnant.'

'Karen. Why didn't you tell me?'

'I was going to tell you when I was certain.'

'That's wonderful news.' Gertie hugged her. 'Does Paul know?'

'Not yet. I'll tell him as soon as it's confirmed. Maybe we'll have a better chance this time.'

10

Molly dragged out the rugs to beat them in the balmy spring air. Clumps of daffodils blazed gold around the trunk of an old oak tree, and the buds of cherry and forsythia trees slowly unfurled in the sunshine. She came back in to get some towels she had piled on the dining-room table, and took them out to dry on the clothes-line. When she had finished, she swept the kitchen floor and put the kettle on for a cup of tea for herself and Biddy. She called Biddy, and when there was no answer went to look for her.

Finally she found her in bed sobbing, head buried in the pillow to stifle her convulsive gasps for breath.

'Biddy? What's happened?'

Biddy lifted her red, swollen eyes and looked at her. 'I can't tell you.'

Molly sat on the bed beside her and took her hand. 'Did you get into trouble with Her Ladyship?'

Biddy shook her head.

'Then tell me . . . it can't be that bad.' Molly wiped Biddy's eyes with a corner of the sheet.

'It's worse.'

'Is it Anthony?'

'Yes.'

'He's had an accident?'

Biddy shook her head and her body shuddered with more suppressed sobs.

'You've got to tell me.'

'I'm pregnant.'

'Oh no.' Molly took her in her arms. 'You'll have to see a doctor.'

Biddy nodded.

'I'll take you.'

'Look at the mess I'm in.' The front of Biddy's dress was wet and crumpled from her tears, and her legs dangled over the side of the bed.

'Oh Biddy, stop crying. I'll help you.'

'How?'

'I'll get a message to Anthony.'

'I don't want to tell him.'

'That's ridiculous, pet. He'll have to know. Sure isn't he the father?'

Biddy sniffed. 'Yes.'

'Stop crying. You'll upset the baby. Now dry your eyes. We'll think of something.'

Biddy's pregnancy made her loneliness for Anthony more acute. In the afternoons, while Thomas slept, she would sit in her room and watch the spring sun dapple the trees. The loneliness would not go away, even when she was peeling vegetables for Molly, or listening to the radio.

Molly took her to the local doctor, who confirmed her pregnancy and advised her to tell her employers. Monica Price sat poker-faced and silent when Biddy told her. Eventually she said, 'And to think it happened while you were living under my roof. I trusted you, Biddy.'

'I never meant it to happen. I didn't honestly think it could.'

'Then you are a fool. I'm afraid I can't keep you on.'

Biddy felt the rejection like a failure. She had let Monica and Thomas down, and she was ashamed.

Monica Price's praise in her reference and the present of a new dress built up Biddy's confidence again, but her heart was broken. She had worked hard running up and down stairs on errands, vacuuming bedrooms, scrubbing floors and moving furniture. Often she had averted a crisis by her resourcefulness and quick response. Monica Price praised her for what she had done for Thomas and herself and told her she had been delighted with her work.

'You can come back to me,' she said, but Biddy knew that her unborn baby was not included in the invitation.

That night she wrote and told Anthony.

Dublin city looked grey with tall buildings as the train pulled into the station. People were milling around the platform, and Biddy's heart pounded as she queued behind other passengers, crumpled from the journey. There was no sign of Anthony. Porters banged doors, shouting to one another. The whistle blew, and the train began to shunt out of the station again, leaving a trail of vapour in its wake. It was getting dark. The crowds dispersed. Still no sign of Anthony. Biddy went into the waiting room and sat by a heater to keep warm. Suddenly he was standing there, smiling at her.

'I thought you weren't coming.'

'What made you think that? I said I'd be here. Come on.' He carried her bag across the platform. They did not speak to each other as he led her out of the station and hailed a taxi. The taxi drew up beside them.

'Rathmines.' Anthony helped Biddy into the back seat, and jumped in beside her, wedging her case between them.

'Where are we going?'

'Friends of mine. The Brophys. They're a nice couple that I stay with sometimes.'

'Where did you meet them?'

'My pal Seán introduced me to them. Ned Brophy's his uncle. You'll be all right with them till I sort something out.'

'Will you be staying there too?'

'No. I have to go to work. But I'll be back in a week. How are you?' He looked anxiously at her. 'You look all right. Have you changed?' He took her hand in his.

'Of course I haven't changed, silly.'

'Have you seen the doctor?'

'Yes.'

'And?'

'I'm definitely pregnant.'

'Oh.' Biddy could see the disappointment in his face. She stared out of the window, not wanting to meet his gaze and the questions in his eyes. In spite of his obvious good humour he looked tired, as if he was weary of life. Only his eyes were fiery.

On reflection Biddy could never remember the streets they drove through, because they all looked similar, and strange. The city centre was bright and the lighted shop windows displayed the most beautiful dresses she had ever seen. Finally the taxi stopped outside a tall, red-bricked house. Anthony jumped out, paid the fare, and carried Biddy's case up to the front door.

A stout woman, her hair in a net, answered it.

'You're here, Anthony. And this must be Biddy.' She put her arm around Biddy and drew her inside. 'It's cold, love. Come and sit by the fire.'

The sitting-room was dark and overcrowded with furniture, but the fire was bright and welcoming. 'Sit down and take the weight off your feet. I'll go and make the tea.'

Anthony sat beside her on the comfortable settee.

'This is a nice place.' Biddy stretched her hands out to the flames.

'She's the best in the world.'

'Are you sure they don't mind?'

''Course not. I told you Ned's a good pal. He was the first one I thought of when I got your letter.'

'It's an awful mess.'

'Can't be helped. We'll sort something out.'

'Like what?'

Mrs Brophy returned with a tray of sandwiches and cakes. A man followed with the teapot.

'This is my husband, Ned.'

'Good evening.' As he shook hands with Biddy, he glanced furtively at Anthony, while his wife urged Biddy to eat something.

'Coming for a pint, Anto?' Ned nodded towards the door.

Anthony looked at Biddy. 'I won't be long. About an hour. Give you a chance to settle in.'

'But I've only just got here.'

Mrs Brophy saw the disappointment in Biddy's face and threw her eyes up to heaven. 'Boys will be boys. Don't mind them, love. You can go to bed early and have a rest. You'll be nice and comfortable here.'

It was a small room with a single bed, a wardrobe and matching dressing-table. As soon as Mrs Brophy had gone back downstairs, Biddy unpacked. She put her powder, lipstick and hairbrush on the dressing-table to help make her feel at home. Outside, traffic noises and the sound of children playing under the street-lamp floated up to her, reminding her of Annie and May. She had to bite her lip to stop herself from crying.

Anthony left the next day, promising Biddy that he would be back in a week. When the week went by and he had not returned, Biddy was not anxious because of his habit of appearing and disappearing. But as the days turned into weeks she became desperate.

'I can't stay on here,' she said to Mrs Brophy. 'I have no money.'

'Don't worry. We'll find work for you,' Mrs Brophy said.

When Mrs Brophy heard that her friends, Maureen and Enzo Carolli, were looking for someone to serve in their bakery shop, she recommended Biddy.

It was a bright, cold morning when Biddy set out for work. Her knees felt wobbly as she walked to the shop on the corner.

'Enzo's Home Bakery' was written on the side wall, in big red lettering. There were other shops along the street, straggled here and there between houses of flats. Biddy's hand shook as she rang the bell.

'Good morning.' A fat man in a long white apron, a white cap covering his black hair, answered the door, then began placing a tray of freshly baked loaves on top of the counter. The smell of the bread made Biddy feel nauseous.

'I'm Biddy Plunkett.'

'Thought you might be. I'm Enzo. There's a shop coat and hat on the peg behind the back door. Maureen will be in later on.'

The coat was several sizes too big, and the hat kept falling sideways. Enzo laughed when he saw her.

'Don't worry. You'll grow into it.'

Biddy went red in the face.

'Start by stacking these loaves in the window. There's always a stampede after seven. Same customers every morning, wanting much the same things. You'll soon get used to it.' He wiped tiny beads of perspiration from his brow. 'You can sweep the floor while you're waiting. And there's a list of our cakes up on the wall you can acquaint yourself with. The prices are written up beside them.' He retreated to the back of the shop.

Enzo rose at five o'clock to bake. He baked in ovens in a back room, and came into the shop only to replenish the shelves. He started with bread, rolls and doughnuts. At eight o'clock he went home for his breakfast and when he returned he baked what he called 'fancy goods': apple tarts, cream horns, jam puffs, sponge sandwiches and fairy cakes.

Customers arrived: postmen, bus conductors, and women on their way to work at a nearby knitwear factory. Maureen came in at eleven, and made tea in the back room.

'You look exhausted,' she said to Biddy. 'Come and have your break before the next customers come in.' She cleared a space at a cluttered table in the corner.

'Have a doughnut.'

Biddy bit into the doughnut. 'This is delicious.'

Maureen pushed the plate in front of her. 'Have another.'

She ate three and had to stop herself from taking a fourth.

Maureen looked at her watch. 'That bloody PJ's late again. I'll kill him.'

'Who's PJ?'

'The delivery boy. Doesn't know the meaning of the word time.'

After the tea-break, Biddy made boxes out of a stack of flat cardboard cut-outs, while Maureen served. A boy of about eighteen, in a brown shop coat, came in whistling.

'You're late.' Maureen gave him a scathing look. 'What kept you?'

'Relax. There's no rush.' Slowly he removed his bicycle clips and, ignoring Maureen, said to Biddy, 'Nice to see a pretty face around here for a change. I'm PJ.'

Biddy said, 'Hello.'

'Enzo will rearrange your face if you don't get Mrs Coleman's order over to her before lunch.'

'There's plenty of time.' His attention returned to Biddy but she was too busy to talk.

Maureen got the orders ready and PJ left. From then until one o'clock Biddy served, boxed and finished off the wrappings with neat bows of gold raffia string.

At half-past twelve Maureen went into the back room, kicked off her shoes and began making sandwiches for their lunch.

PJ returned singing, 'Kisses sweeter than wine. Oh oh, kisses sweeter than wine.'

He took his place at the table. 'Mrs Sherman should be feeling sweet. Two dozen iced buns and a dozen cream horns kissed her fat lips this morning.'

'They weren't all for her. She had a bridge party,' Maureen said. 'Did you give Mrs Pemberton her bill?'

'Forgot.' He took a slurp of tea from a large mug, then removed a jumble of scraps of paper entangled in a comb from his breast pocket. He smoothed them out with the palm of his hand.

'All done,' he declared.

'Except Pemberton's account. She owes a fortune. And when you get back, sweep the floor and tidy up the storeroom.'

'Who's the new tart? Fine thing anyways.'

'Biddy Plunkett is her name and I'll thank you to show a bit of respect. She's a young lady.'

'Game ball. A nice bit of crumpet, so she is.' He winked at Biddy as she came in, swaying on her feet with fatigue.

'Get a move on,' Enzo said to PJ, the morning paper in his hand and a pencil stuck behind his ear. 'No time for dallying. Get that order over to Mrs Pemberton. She'll be waiting. And give her the bill.'

'Fat slob,' PJ swore under his breath. 'If she eats any more doughnuts she'll burst. Sure her backside's the breadth of the van. She should be on a seaside postcard.'

'I told you before not to make personal remarks about the customers,' Maureen said.

'It's only the truth.' PJ got to his feet. 'No rest for the wicked.'

'You can have an hour off after lunch,' Maureen said to Biddy. 'It'll be quiet till four.'

'I wouldn't mind an hour off meself.' PJ stretched and yawned. 'It's a long day.'

'Get cracking.' Maureen clapped her hands and he made a mock run for the door.

Biddy removed her shoes as soon as she sat down.

'Is it always this busy?' she asked.

'Always. And sometimes we've deliveries up until eight o'clock at night.'

'So PJ's worked off his feet,' Biddy laughed.

'He works hard, to be fair. If only we could get him in earlier in the mornings.'

Biddy settled in. After work she ate the dinner Mrs Brophy had prepared for her, and went to bed too exhausted to listen to the wireless. She wrote to her mother telling her that she had moved to Dublin to a better job, but did not give her address.

One evening, a few days after Biddy had started working there, a neat wiry man came into the shop and asked for Enzo. He drummed his fingers on the counter while he waited. Biddy, standing back from him, could see that he was in an angry mood. PJ stopped what he was doing and stared at him.

Enzo appeared, followed by Maureen.

The man produced a bill. 'My name is Pemberton and this account is wrong.'

Enzo took the bill from his hand, and looked at it.

'I'll report you, me boy,' the man continued. 'Not content with all the money you're making, you have to extract the last few shillings from the likes of us, who are eejits enough to give it to you.'

Enzo leaned over the counter, a malicious grin on his face.

'You can't come in here throwing your weight around. Not only is this bill correct, it's also overdue. What's more, I'm not standing for it any longer. You can pay up.'

'I'll do no such thing. I'm fed up getting rooked by you.'

'I'll see you in court.'

'You can see me in hell for all the good it'll do you.' Pemberton went to leave the shop. 'You've got all you're getting from me.'

'Wait a minute.' Enzo ran into the back room and returned with a red ledger. He turned the pages, and carefully pointed to each item entered in red ink. 'There's that order, and that, and do you see that?' He pointed his finger at figures underscored at the bottom of a column of figures.

'Not possible,' Pemberton said.

'Here. See for yourself.' Before Pemberton could say another word Enzo shoved the ledger into his face.

'Carried forward here. Carried forward there. Look.'

There was a terrible silence. Mr Pemberton stood stock still. Then, reaching out, he grabbed the book, and stared at the figures, his lips clenched as if he did not trust himself to speak.

'Now do you believe me?'

Pemberton shut the ledger with a bang, and heaved his chest as if he were about to cry. Suddenly he let out a roar. 'She'll be sorry for this. I'll kill her!'

Everyone stared. Biddy was afraid she was going to faint.

'I've been threatening it for long enough, but this time she's done it. I'll kill her.' He ran from the shop, fists clenched, face the colour of blood.

Maureen put her hand across her mouth. 'Oh good God, he'll swing for her. Send PJ to warn her.'

'This is one row I'm keeping out of,' Enzo said.

'I'll have to phone her.' Maureen headed towards the rear of the shop.

'Let them at it,' Enzo called after her.

'He's mean with money. Never gives her enough,' Maureen called back.

'Then she shouldn't run up bills.'

'She's afraid of him,' Maureen replied.

'And the size of her!' Enzo laughed.

PJ looked incredulous. 'What about the size of him? Sure a handy woman could wash him on a saucer.'

11

Biddy worked in the bakery until she could hide her pregnancy under her smock no longer. Two months before her baby was due, Maureen offered to go and tell her mother. May answered the door and said that her mother was working and would be back soon.

'Can I wait?'

'Yes.' May took her into the kitchen. She paced the floor while she waited for Mrs Plunkett to return. When she heard the key in the lock, she went into the hall to meet her.

'Hello, Mrs Plunkett. I'm Maureen, a friend of Biddy's.'

'Oh yes.' Mrs Plunkett eyed her suspiciously while removing her hat and coat. 'What's up then?' She looked closely at Maureen as she passed into the kitchen. 'You look as if you've seen a ghost . . .'

'I'm afraid it's bad news,' Maureen said more abruptly than she intended.

'Oh God. Is Biddy all right? Has she lost her job?'

'It's worse than that.'

'What is it?'

Maureen faced her. 'Biddy's pregnant.'

'Pregnant.' She repeated the word as if she were hearing it for the first time. 'Biddy pregnant. That's ridiculous. Sure she's only a child.'

'I'm afraid it's true.'

Mrs Plunkett sat down suddenly. 'Not Biddy. She couldn't be. She wouldn't. She's more sense. Sure isn't she sick of minding them?' She stared at the table as fury replaced horror and lit up her eyes. Then she looked up at Maureen. 'How do you know?'

'She told me.' Maureen paused. 'In fact she asked me to tell you.'

'Oh God. Oh my sweet Jesus. Who's the father?' She banged her fist on the table. 'Who is he?'

'Anthony Quinn.'

'Oh Christ in his heaven.' She rose from the table and paced the floor. 'I might have known. I should have guessed straight away. That lout. He was never any good. Always in trouble. 'Tis the likes of him would stop at nothing to get a decent girl into trouble. Destroy her character.'

She sat down again. Maureen went to her and put a restraining hand on her worn sleeve. Mrs Plunkett looked around the kitchen. 'What's going to happen to us all? Where's her father now? Look at me. Working and praying all my life and no one to do a hand's turn. I mean, look at us. What have I ever done to deserve this? What'll people say? What'll the neighbours think? What'll Father Breen say? I'll have to go and see him. Oh my God, he'll damn her from the pulpit and we'll be disgraced in our own town.' Her voice rose in hysteria.

'It isn't that bad, Mrs Plunkett. It's not a disease.'

'It's worse. She's a damned soul. Blackened in hell for the rest of her life. I'm the mother of a sinner.' She clasped her knees and rocked herself back and forth, distressing herself more and more as she talked. 'And where'll she go?'

'I thought you might let her come home.'

Mrs Plunkett did not seem to hear her. 'Yes. That's the next thing. As if I haven't enough on my plate.'

'We'll work something out. It's not the end of the world.'

'Where's Anthony Quinn?'

'Biddy hasn't heard from him for a while. She thinks he's working in England.'

'You mark my words, she won't either.'

In the end Biddy had no choice but to return home to Dun Laoghaire. Mrs Plunkett called Anthony a sly fox, but it was nothing to the tirade of abuse she lashed out on her daughter.

'How could you let him do that to you? As if we didn't have enough problems. God almighty what are we going to do?' Her voice was at screaming pitch. Biddy backed away.

'Where did you meet that young hooligan anyway? I thought you were safe in Price's house.'

'He came to see me there. Took me out.' Biddy put her hand across the bulge of her stomach in a protective gesture.

'And he told you he loved you, and you, you silly fool, fell for it.'

'It wasn't like that.'

'Don't interrupt. You think you know everything. You know nothing.'

'That's your fault.' The words were out of Biddy's mouth before she had time to stop them.

'Oh, it's all *my* fault now.'

'Sorry. I didn't mean it.'

'Sit down and shut up.'

Biddy sat down.

'You listen to me. It wasn't bad enough that your father walked out on us. Now I have to deal with this.'

Biddy closed her eyes.

'What would your father say now? Answer me that, you that has all the answers.'

Biddy shrugged helplessly. An image of her father's face flashed through her mind. 'Daddy would ask me if I were happy. If I loved Anthony, and if he loved me.'

Her mother raised her hand and slapped her across the face.

'Your daddy would ask you no such thing. Your daddy wouldn't care enough. He didn't care when he left us, did he?' She lashed out again, stinging Biddy's face with the palm of her hand. Biddy leaned back in an attempt to avoid another blow. The chair swayed and keeled over. She fell to the ground. A pain flashed through her stomach. She attempted to rise, but her mother pinned her to the ground with both hands.

'What are you going to do to me?'

'Leave her alone!' May stood at the door crying.

Her mother rose. 'I haven't finished with you yet, my girl. For the moment I'll let Father Breen deal with you. He'll know what to do.'

Biddy got to her feet.

Her mother lit a cigarette. 'I can tell you this much. You'll come to a bad end. Carrying on with the likes of Anthony Quinn. And me sending you away to get rid of him. You got what you deserved. Get out of my sight.'

Biddy ran upstairs to her bedroom. Her mother shouted after her, 'Don't come down again until I get the priest.'

Biddy buried her face in the comfort of her pillow. Crying, trembling, she lay there, her arms wrapped around her helpless body.

'Biddy . . . Biddy?' May's voice was gentle in the darkness. 'Are you all right, Biddy?'

'Yes, 'course I am.'

May went to her, and folded her in her arms, in the comforting gesture so familiar to them both. 'What happened?'

'It's all right, love. Don't worry.'

'I like Anthony. He's nice.'

They stayed together like that for the rest of the night.

Biddy kept out of her mother's way and tried not to think about Anthony, but she could not get him out of her mind. Her love for him, and the discomfort of her pregnancy, made life unbearable. She became silent, remembering the change in his eyes when he had met her at the station; eyes that were once amused and bright were suddenly shrewd and alert.

Ita Plunkett went to see the parish priest and it was his intervention that sent Biddy on her lonely journey to the Magdalen Convent in Donnybrook.

'It's the best place for her. The nuns are charitable and trained in the care of young girls like Biddy. She'll be well looked after, and given work to do,' he said to Mrs Plunkett.

'It's the ideal solution, Father.'

Father Breen was so happy that Mrs Plunkett had approved of his suggestion that he offered to take Biddy to the Magdalen Laundry himself. They arrived at the grey stone building opposite Donnybrook church late in the afternoon.

When Father Breen stopped to open the tall gates, Biddy noticed the iron bars on the windows. They entered by a side door, and walked down a stone-flagged passage.

A nun came to meet them, the skirts of her habit pinned up.

'Good afternoon, Sister Attracta.' Father Breen smiled congenially. 'This is young Biddy Plunkett.'

The nun bowed her head slightly as she greeted the

priest then looked at Biddy. Her face was small in the frame of her white veil, and her skin glistened. She took Biddy's hand in her cold one.

'You'll be safe here,' she said. 'No question of any misbehaviour. And you'll soon settle down. Plenty to do. Isn't that right, Father?'

'Indeed. A guaranteed job. What more could you want?'

Biddy was taken along a series of long corridors, with Sister Attracta unlocking and locking every door as they went. They came to an enormous, high-ceilinged room that smelt of soap. Scrupulously clean sinks stretched lengthwise along the walls. Young girls and women were working quietly together. Some were carrying baskets full of washing, others were scrubbing clothes, or wringing them through mangles. Most of them were wearing blue housecoats, and those in their own clothes were shabbily dressed. A few girls, bunched together at the end of the room talking, dispersed as Sister Attracta approached.

She walked up and down, her black rosary beads swinging from her waist, inspecting the basins. Biddy was left standing by herself. Slowly the girls looked towards her, their eyes withdrawn and hesitant, as if she were hardly worth their gaze. Biddy studied the tiled floor. A girl of about twenty, with short straight hair and vacant eyes, came over to her.

'I'm Mona,' she said. 'If you follow me, I'll get you an overall and show you what to do.'

She led the way to a cloakroom. While Biddy hung up her coat and donned a blue overall, Mona kept her eyes averted as if to discourage any conversation. She walked ahead of Biddy back to the laundry-room, and remained detached as she filled a basin, testing the water temperature with red lumpy hands. Then she took out washing from a linen bag.

'Separate the whites first.' Arms raised, she began rubbing Sunlight soap into the clothes, then gathered them in bunches to knead against the scrubbing board.

'Got it?'

'Yes.'

'Here. You have a go.'

Biddy hesitated, afraid of making a mistake. Mona pushed her hands down into the water with her own damp ones.

'They're only clothes. They won't bite. Carry on. I'll be back.'

The girl at the next basin turned to Biddy. Hair in disarray, her face shining with perspiration, she said, 'What happened to your fella? Did he scarper?'

Inexplicable shame flushed Biddy's face, and then a surge of anger shot through her.

'Mind your own business,' she retorted and concentrated on her washing.

The other girl sucked in her breath in irritation. Mona returned to check Biddy's progress.

'Not bad. The shirt collars are the worst. And you can't

use a scrubbing brush; frays them.' She rifled through the bag of washing.

'There's a good headscarf. Wash it separately or the colours will run.'

Mona's voice grew more exasperated as she went along.

A bell rang for tea. The girls, tired and dishevelled, sat opposite one another at long tables in the refectory. One eventually said to Biddy, 'Have some bread and margarine. It tastes awful, but you'll get used to it.'

'If you're hungry enough, you'll eat it,' said a girl with fuzzy hair and cold blue eyes. 'Where are you from anyway?'

'Dun Laoghaire.'

'I was in Dun Laoghaire once to see me fella off to England. Never came back neither,' she sighed. 'The story of our lives. Want a cup of tea?' Taking a little brown bag from her pocket she said, 'My rations. You'll get yours tomorrow.'

'Aren't you cold?' Biddy asked when she saw that the girl was not wearing stockings.

'I haven't had a pair of stockings since I was sixteen. Got a boyfriend?'

Biddy nodded.

'Haven't seen a boy since I came here.'

'How long ago was that?'

'Three years. And there isn't much chance of meeting one in here.'

She poured weak tea into Biddy's cup.

★　★　★

In her bed, in the long dormitory at the top of the convent, Biddy's view was of slanting roofs with rotting tiles. Barbed wire topped the railings. As soon as the lights went out, she heard the key turn in the lock. Someone started talking.

A voice hissed, 'Be quiet.'

Another voice called out, 'Who's going to make me?'

'I'll break your face.'

'Shut up the pair of you. Some of us want to sleep.'

Bewildered, Biddy tucked her head under her pillow to escape the row. Too exhausted to think, she fell into a merciful sleep that temporarily released her pain.

The next day she was assigned to take the nuns' ironing upstairs to the ironing room.

'Sister's pet,' a sour-faced girl with brown eyes mocked, as Biddy carefully folded the nuns' garments.

'Why?' Biddy asked in surprise.

'Only the privileged handle the nuns' laundry. You must be sucking up to Sister Attracta.'

Biddy ignored her and went upstairs.

A girl of about eighteen sprawled in a chair in the ironing room. She was a mountain of flesh. Her swollen feet spilled out over worn flat shoes, and enormous legs spread up under her blue overall to join the folds of flab that rolled over her belly. A cigarette was burning between her lips. She finished her cup of tea and belched. White linen garments were folded and neatly stacked on the table behind.

'Hello. I'm Biddy Plunkett.'

'I heard we had a new one. What're you staring at?'

'Sorry.' Biddy cast down her eyes.

'I'm not pregnant, if that's what you're thinking. I work for the nuns.'

'I didn't mean to stare.'

'Everyone does. Something wrong with my glands they say. By the way, my name is Nancy. Did you bring up all the washing?'

'Yes. Everything's dry.'

'Now you must hang out more clothes before sundown.

'In the evening when the sun goes down,' she sang as she heaved herself out of her chair and faced the pile of ironing.

'Isn't it too late?'

'It's never late here,' she sighed. 'You can't stand it, can you love?'

'No.'

'Want a glass of lemonade?' Nancy went to the cupboard and took out two small bottles of Savage Smyth, prising the caps off with her teeth.

'Here.' Her smile widened as she watched Biddy's eyes light up.

'Thanks. Where did you get these?'

'I have a way with the nuns. I take very special care of their ironing. Attracta says I'm the best they've ever had. See for yourself.'

White linen garments were folded and neatly stacked on a table beside an ironing-board. There was more ironing, still warm to the touch, on hangers. The room smelt of lavender, starch, and altar breads.

'Lucky you.'

'Don't take any notice of those pinched-up nuns. They're always holding back, afraid to let their feelings show. I've known them for years.'

Nancy moved the tip of the iron expertly into the seams of the dampened starched cotton. It tightened and stretched under the heat.

'If I had a penny for every piece of clothing I iron, I'd be rich. Those nuns' wimples are the devil. My sweat went into the ironing of them until they were threadbare.'

'Why don't you get a job somewhere?'

'I'm not trained for anything. I've been here since I was fifteen, and I'm my own boss, in a way. You come up here sometimes. I might have a piece of chocolate or an extra bit of tea or sugar for your ration bag.'

'I'll only get into trouble.'

'I'll watch out for you.'

Suddenly Biddy wanted to hug the broad arms that ironed and hung the nuns' clothes on hangers.

'I'm always starving,' Biddy said, sipping her lemonade.

'Everybody here is starving, love. You're very young, Biddy, but you'll be all right. I can tell. You're strong.'

'I know I'll be all right,' Biddy said, 'because I've no intention of staying.'

'I see.' Nancy drained her lemonade bottle and, with

a twist of her wrist, tossed it out of the window. It smashed on the far roof, sending shards of glass sliding down the tiles.

'You'll be killed.'

'Let old Higgins clear it up. If it doesn't fall on his baldy head and split it first.'

Laughter rippled through her, shaking her enormous body. She dried her eyes with the back of her hand. 'We can't do much, but there's no law against laughing.'

'If I write a letter, will you post it for me?'

'If I had a penny for every letter I posted to the boyfriends. 'Course I will.'

That night Biddy wrote to Gertie asking her to come to see her.

The laundry-room was vast, enclosed, secret and mostly silent. The girls washed and rinsed, their bodies dragging and shifting with the exertion of getting the last drop of grey water out of the clothes. There was something satisfying about removing all the dirt, running the washed clothes through clear water, then through a mangle. The mangle had double rubber rollers that squeezed the clothes between them. Trapped air ballooned the material and jets of water squirted out as the handle was turned. That was the part of the ritual that Biddy liked. Pegging out the washing to stiffen in the breeze gave her a respite from the sweat of the laundry.

Mona was in charge of the stores, which were kept in a

small room lined with shelves and crammed with packages of washing powder, Robin starch, blue bags to whiten the whites, bars of Sunlight soap, carbolic soap and bleach. A docket had to be written out by Mona, and then signed by the recipient. Biddy hated that procedure.

Soon Biddy got to know the Magdalen girls and the women who were known as 'penitents'. Women who had given birth out of wedlock and were seeking God's forgiveness. They kept their distance, had more responsible jobs, and lived the rule with the nuns, attending Mass and special prayers with them, and singing in their choir.

12

'Child.'

Biddy was hanging out the washing one day when she turned to see the old nun who usually sat under the shelter of the oak tree beckoning to her. The sun was shining on the first warm spring day, and her eyes were on the movements of the girls who came and went through the back door.

Biddy went to her.

Fumbling with her embroidery, the old nun said, 'Sit down here beside me and unravel the strands of that pink skein for me.'

'Yes, Mother.' Biddy handed her the pink.

'Now the blue. I'll need another skein soon. I'm running out of blue.'

'It's beautiful,' Biddy remarked as she watched the slow, arthritic hands work magnificent stitches into the material. 'Where did you learn to do that?'

'Embroidery is part of our training. The altar robes, the serving cloths, the priests' vestments are all embroidered by the nuns as a testament to God's great glory and His Holy

Will. But I'm getting old, child, and these stitches are getting slower and more painful.'

The laundry door opened and Biddy stood up. 'I'd better go.'

'You remind me of myself when I was a slip of a girl. Come and see me tomorrow.'

'If I can.' Biddy returned to the laundry to continue scrubbing, squeezing, mangling, hanging out and folding.

Old Mother Catherine waited for Biddy every fine day, sitting under the tree, wrapped up against the harsh spring breeze, working stitches round scalloped edges. Biddy would come and sit with her for a little while. They became fast friends.

'What's your hurry? Can't you stay and talk a while?' the old nun would protest when Biddy got up to leave.

'Yes, Mother. I mean no, I can't. I have another bucket of washing to hang out, and more steeping in the sink.'

'Let it wait. The washing won't disappear.'

'Don't I know. And the worst of it is that it's never finished.'

'It's something to be grateful for, child. It's work. Where would you be without it?'

'Down at the beach with the tide lapping around my toes. Or reading a book.'

'Of course you will. This place isn't the be all and end all.'

'It is to us. We'll never get out of here.' Biddy's eyes watched girls taking buckets of washing to the clothes-lines.

'The place will fall some day and nobody will be any the wiser that we were here. My dreams came to nothing, but it's not too late for you.'

'I'd like to get out of here, but I've nowhere to go.' Biddy scratched the sores on her head.

'Don't let that deter you. You're young and strong. There's plenty of work in you yet. Look at your hands. Red and sore from the washing. I'll have to give you a bit of cream.' She took one of Biddy's hands in her calloused ones. 'And your nails are bitten to the quick. Your hair's too short.'

'Sister Attracta cut it yesterday because of my scabs.'

'A rub of borax ointment. That'll do the trick. Don't let your appearance go.'

'What's the point? I spend all my time washing clothes. Who'll ever see me anyway?'

'You have the face of an angel, and skin like dewdrops. And your whole life in front of you. Me, I have only the dead.'

Over the weeks Mother Catherine told Biddy stories about her life. One day she said, 'I was happy when I entered; full of God and expectations. I was part of a group being trained to teach, with enough to eat and a roof over my head. Happy and prayerful, working among the poor. My prayers had been answered.'

Her eyes were on her needle as she sewed. Eventually she said, 'Looking back, I realize that, far from being poor, the church was rich. Probably because of poor people like you, working for nothing.'

'I'm sure you'll live for a long time yet.'

'Don't be alarmed. I'm not afraid of death. I'm looking forward to it. Heaven seems a more attractive alternative to me. Help me up, child; I must go in. It's getting cold. Come to see me tomorrow if it's fine.'

Stooped and slow, she made her way along the path, her embroidery bag clutched in her hand.

Biddy ran back to the laundry and resumed her work without a word to anyone. No one seemed to have missed her.

A few weeks later Sister Attracta handed Biddy a letter.

'Father Breen was here this morning and asked me to give you this from your mother.'

Biddy thanked her and went to the toilet to read it in private. She was surprised to find that it was from Gertie.

Dear Biddy,

I hope you are getting on all right and not finding the work too hard. We are all thinking of you and hope you are keeping well, and that God will grant you a safe delivery.

Lizzie wrote yesterday to tell us all about her wedding plans. As I knew you would be interested in hearing the news, I enclose her letter. I also enclose an invitation for you to see what they look like, and a pound note to buy yourself some stockings. Karen, Paul and John have returned to the States to visit Paul's parents before the wedding, so things are very quiet.

All are well here. Mrs Keogh is helping out at Father

*Breen's, but she'll be back full-time in the summer. I have
kept your job for you in the hope that you will be able to
return to us. I met your mother at Mass on Sunday and she
seems to be in good form, as are Annie and May.*

*Keep up the heart and write and let us know how you
are, or if there is anything that you want. Bill and John send
their love.*

Yours sincerely,

Gertie Doyle

Biddy folded the letter and returned it to its envelope.
Carefully she took out the white card and studied the
silver doves and cupids entwining garlands of flowers around
the silver embossed words:

WEDDING INVITATION

Slowly she opened the card, and turned the delicate page
to read the scrolled writing:

*Mr and Mrs William Doyle
request the pleasure of the company of*

---

*at the marriage of their daughter
Elizabeth Mary*

to

*Mr Peter James Scanlon
at St Patrick's Church, Queens, New York*

on
Saturday, 4 June 1951
at 11:00 a.m.
and afterwards at a reception in
The Park Hotel
Queens
New York

Santa Maria   *R.S.V.P. by*
Victoria Terrace   *21 May 1951*
Dun Laoghaire
Co. Dublin

It was the first time that Biddy had ever seen a wedding invitation. Gertie had enclosed the letter from Lizzie that had accompanied the invitation. Full of details, it described her meeting with the monsignor who was to marry them, booking the hotel, hiring the wedding cars, and all the early preparations for such an important occasion.

Biddy replaced the letters in the envelope and hid it in the pocket of her overall. Later on she would hide it under the mattress of her bed. Conscious of time passing, she hurried back to the laundry-room and spent the rest of the day dreaming of Lizzie's wedding in New York and wishing she could be there.

There was another girl, named Grace, who worked for the nuns. She was pretty, with long hair that shone. She got paid for her labour, so she was rich in the eyes of the Magdalen girls. Her clothes were better than theirs and her shoes were made of soft leather that sometimes squeaked. She wore angora sweaters and pleated skirts under her housecoat, and walked with authority, her head held high.

Grace Brown enthralled the entire laundry. The nuns always smiled at her. The penitents stepped to one side to let her pass, and when she assigned work to the laundry girls, they did not sigh with irritation, or snigger behind her back. When she went to one of their sinks with washing, they genuflected with their eyes. At meal-times they flocked around her to hear her tell stories about life in the outside world, or to describe the latest film she had seen. She would dispense her food or some treat she had brought from home. Often she would give them the cup of tea from her tray, and they would sip it in turns.

Biddy's fascination with Grace was obvious in her demeanour. She prayed that Grace would befriend her, so she could hold conversations with her; perhaps listen to her soft voice telling her about her mother, brothers and sisters.

Apart from her friendship with Nancy and Grace, Biddy's other interest was her baby. She would talk to it like a friend. Knowing that lifting the washing was not good for it, she would say, 'Be patient now. It'll all be over in a few weeks.'

She accepted the discomfort of carrying it, and the scabs that spread when she itched her head, because there was someone keeping her company in that prison. There were times when she cursed Anthony and her mother for the position in which she found herself. Times of such great loneliness and pain that she longed to run away, and was determined to do so some day.

Grace put ointment on Biddy's sores and, when they did not heal, she went to Sister Attracta.

'You'll have to do something, Sister. She's scratching her head and spreading them.'

Sister Attracta sent for Biddy and examined her head.

'Grace will take you to the chemist this afternoon. Mr Maguire will have a look at those sores before you spread them among the other girls.'

She eyed the holes in Biddy's stretched brown stockings. 'You'll have to tidy yourself up. I'll get you another pair of stockings. Be as inconspicuous as you possibly can. We don't want any unnecessary attention drawn to you.'

It was a bright day after a week of rain. Puddles dried up quickly in the sun. Biddy pulled the loose coat Sister Attracta had lent her around her stomach, and with her face half-hidden in her headscarf, walked with Grace to the shops.

'Hey goodlookin',' a boy on a bike called to Grace.

Grace ignored him. Lips set in a smile, she linked Biddy as they walked on.

'Take no notice.'

She began telling Biddy about the picture she had seen

the previous night, *That Midnight Kiss*, starring Mario Lanza and Kathryn Grayson.

'It's the first time I've ever seen Mario Lanza and I've fallen in love with him. He's a great singer, and so handsome. I'm going to go to every picture he's in from now on.'

Walking with Grace, enjoying both the warm spring breeze and the freedom of the street, made Biddy forget her misery.

'Some day I'm going to have nice clothes like yours, and go to the cinema,' Biddy said.

'Sure you will, lovey. But first let's get you better.'

Mr Maguire gave Biddy a tube of ointment. 'Use this sparingly and it'll do the trick.'

He took Grace to one side. 'Tell Sister Attracta she's to drink plenty of milk and eat more vegetables. It's lack of nourishment. And take her this for the head lice. That girl's hair is crawling.'

'I'll tell her all right,' Grace said. 'I don't know if it'll do any good though.'

On the way back, Grace took Biddy into an ice-cream parlour. They sat choosing flavours from the menu: banana, strawberry, raspberry, chocolate and toffee. Biddy, eager to taste them all, felt that the scabs on her head hardly merited such a treat.

Grace took a dainty purse from her pocket. 'What'll you have?'

'Whatever you think's the nicest.'

'Two cream sodas with raspberry ripple,' Grace said when the waitress came. Biddy's eyes watered with pleasure as she scooped the ice-cream off the spoon with her tongue.

'When is the baby due?' Grace asked.

'In about six weeks. I can't wait to see it.'

'I feel sorry for the girls. Most of them don't know anything about life, never mind being man-mad like people think they are.'

'I want to keep my baby,' Biddy blurted out. Then she seemed to fold into herself, as if regretting that she had spoken out.

'Of course you do. It's not possible though.' Grace took her hand, her eyes misty.

'We'll see.' Biddy told Grace about her secret ambition to become a fashion designer and dress the rich and famous.

Grace did not laugh.

Passing the Post Office on the way back to the laundry, Biddy noticed a pay phone inside the door.

'Grace, can you lend me a threepenny bit to use the phone? I'd like to talk to my mother.'

'Has your mother got a phone?'

'There's one where she works.'

Grace handed her the money. 'Don't tell anyone I let you, and don't be long. I'll keep watch.' Grace guarded the phone box while Biddy rang Santa Maria. Mrs Keogh answered.

'Is Mrs Doyle there please?'

'No. Who is it?'

Biddy hesitated. Finally she said, 'Biddy. Will you give her a message for me please?'

'What?' Curiosity suddenly overcame Mrs Keogh's better judgement.

'Will you ask her to contact me please?' The phone went dead.

The pains started early one morning, when Biddy was hunched over a sinkful of washing. They were not too bad, but Grace insisted on taking her to a big room she had never been in before. There was a row of beds with curtains around them, and a wash–hand basin in the corner. A little old nun named Mother Dymphna examined her.

'Everything's in order. You won't have any trouble,' she told Biddy. Then she turned to Grace. 'I'll keep her here.'

There had been no preparation for childbirth: no books to read, no classes to attend. Biddy often thought afterwards that, even if there had been, nothing could have prepared her for the experience.

As the morning progressed, the pain moved outwards from the pit of her stomach, and she had to double over until it passed. When it receded, she would relax, thinking it had gone altogether, but gradually it would return, forming its own rhythm, like the beating of a drum. Slow to begin with, moving upwards and outwards, until her whole body was immersed in it.

When she thought she could stand it no longer, it would subside, only to begin its slow insidious dance again, rising to a crescendo until she was left gasping for breath. Between bouts she would lie still.

The pauses became less frequent. Frightened, she called out for help. Mother Dymphna hovered, alternately soothing and coaxing. Biddy tried to sleep, and did for a little while. Suddenly she woke up bathed in perspiration. Her body felt as if it was in the grip of some outside force. She cried out, her mind becoming so confused with pain that it removed her fear. Her control snapped. Hands held her down. Cloths cooled her face. She screamed.

'Don't push.' The quiet voice of Mother Dymphna counted each breath out loud. Biddy's body tensed with the resistance of the greatest urge to push she would ever have in her life.

'I can't do it,' she gasped as the pain subsided.

'You're doing it.' Mother Dymphna wiped her face with a damp cloth.

Suddenly the pain returned, dragging her downwards.

'Now push, Biddy.'

There was a rush of something warm and wet, then an easeful sliding away.

'A healthy baby girl. God is good. You've done well.'

Mother Dymphna laid the baby on her chest. Biddy held her carefully. She was not as she had imagined. Her enormous eyes were uncomprehending, her mouth tiny and vulnerable. It twitched when she began to cry, then roar, filling her new lungs with oxygen. Biddy cradled her downy head and kissed her swollen eyelids. The scrap of humanity that was her daughter nestled into her arms, stopped crying and made sucking noises, working her mouth ceaselessly.

'I think she's hungry.'

'I'll take her to the nursery.' Mother Dymphna saw the haunted expression on Biddy's face, as she took her baby away.

'You will bring her back?'

'Try and get some sleep now.'

Biddy was ill for several days with fever. Sister Attracta came to see her.

'You're grand now, Biddy, thank God.'

'Where's my baby?' Biddy's eyes searched her face.

'Shhhh. Don't upset yourself.'

Panic made Biddy's voice rise and reverberate around the room. 'Why don't you bring her to me? It's ages since I've seen her.'

'You'll be all right. You're having a bad day.'

Biddy tried to lift herself up. Sister Attracta's hands held her arms, her fingernails digging into her flesh.

As soon as she began to recover, Biddy persecuted Mother Dymphna until she let her feed and change the baby. She would linger over the feed as long as she could, and take ages to change her. During that time she would tell her fairy tales or nursery rhymes. Sometimes she sang to her. Often she would advise her about good behaviour: 'Respect yourself, study hard, learn new things to better yourself.' Her cautionary tales were poignant because the baby she held in the crook of her arm was the heartbreak she sang about.

Biddy's baby had inherited Anthony's eyes. They were cornflower blue, flecked with gold lights. And she had Biddy's mother's straight nose. Had circumstances been different, Biddy was certain that her mother would have been proud of her granddaughter.

Biddy told her all about Anthony, and his ambition to be a world-famous boxer. She explained to her how things had gone badly wrong for her daddy, mainly because of his bad temper. 'Life is hard,' she whispered into the shell-pink ear. 'I won't be able to right the wrongs for you, or take on your battles. But I'll be there for you, especially when you're frightened.'

When her baby was two weeks old, Anthony came to see her. She could remember him crossing the room, awkwardly putting his arms around her. She watched him with terrible detachment, conscious of nothing, especially not of the future.

'I came as soon as I could. We'll get married.'

Amazed, she looked at him. Then freeing herself from him, she said, 'I need time to think.'

'I'll come back when you feel better.' His eyes were soft, almost tender, but nervousness cracked his voice.

'I think it would be better if you stayed away for a while.'

His brow furrowed. 'How long?'

'For a while anyway. I want time to think. Sort myself out.'

He wrote to her telling her that he would visit her again soon, and she replied, inventing excuses not to see him. She wanted desperately not to be hurt again, to make the right choice. The influence her waning passion had on him was that he wanted to see her all the more.

When she recovered, she continued to work, and was given permission to sit with Mother Catherine occasionally. How many hours she knelt in the chapel praying, or scrubbing the wood block floors, she never knew; hours of prayers, and sacrifice, hours waiting, for what she was not sure.

She continued to feed and change her baby, because there was no one else to do it. Mother Dymphna reminded her regularly that it was only until they found a suitable home. One day she sneaked the baby down to the chapel, wrapped in a shawl, to show her to Mother Catherine.

'I want you to be her godmother.'

'I'm too old. I'd never see her growing up.'

'It's *now* she needs you.' Biddy put the baby into her arms. 'I'd like to call her Catherine after you.'

Mother Catherine held the baby close. 'I'll arrange it.' She kissed the baby's forehead and Biddy took her back to the nursery.

Her love for Anthony was now a solitary passion which evaporated in the steam and sweat of the laundry-room. There was no apology from the nuns when the rivulets of perspiration trickled down her face, or when her back ached from the weight of the huge baskets. They told her that she was exemplary and that she would be rewarded in heaven for her efforts.

Anthony stayed away for several weeks. When he did turn up one day she did not say, 'Where have you been?'

'Have you thought about us getting married?' he asked.

Biddy, realising that he liked being free and was not ready to settle down, said she needed more time to decide.

Anthony looked puzzled. 'Can I see the baby?'

'Sister Attracta won't hear of it.'

'Why? It's my baby too.'

'She won't say why.'

'When we're married, they'll have to let us have the baby.'

'I don't want you to marry me because you feel you have to. I want you to want us both.'

'I do. I love you, Biddy. I've always loved you, and I'll love the baby too if you give me a chance. I want to take care of you both.'

Biddy was not convinced.

Sister Attracta came into the room, her man's watch in her hand, and stood waiting while Anthony said good-bye.

Biddy was given the task of marking the laundry list with Nancy every evening, before the delivery man called to collect the enormous baskets.

'Any word from your fella?' Nancy asked as Biddy knelt over the basket, checking each item that Nancy called out from a list.

'No,' Biddy said, realizing for the first time that Anthony had not written for three weeks. When she had filled the basket with fresh laundry, Sister Attracta sent for her.

'Your mother is here to see you.'

Biddy followed her to one of the nuns' parlours.

Mrs Plunkett's face seemed smaller, her features more pointed. She was sitting beside a table, head bent, arms folded in her lap.

Biddy said, 'Hello Mam,' and immediately got tongue-tied.

'Biddy.'

'Mam, I want to keep my baby.'

There was silence. A look of exhaustion came over her mother's face. 'You're only a child yourself.'

Sister Attracta said, 'You have a long time ahead of you before you're fit to be a mother.'

Biddy looked pleadingly at her mother. 'Couldn't I bring her home? I'd be able to look after her.'

'Are you mad? I reared you lot. That was enough. Sister tells me there's no word of Anthony.'

Biddy looked at Sister Attracta. 'Not for a while.'

'Thought as much. Now you'll have to give the baby up.'

'I'll get a job somewhere that'll take her as well.'

'That would be nothing short of a miracle, child,' Sister Attracta said. 'Come to the chapel and we'll pray together for a good home for the little one.'

As they walked along the corridor, Sister Attracta said to Biddy, 'Remember you are a child of God, and God does not let his children down. We will pray that He will find an earthly father and mother for your child, until she is reunited with her heavenly parents. We must hope and pray and keep the faith.'

The chapel was quiet. Biddy's shoes squeaked on the polished floor as she genuflected. She blessed herself and knelt down. Sister Attracta knelt beside her.

'Pray, Biddy, pray. Tomorrow everything will look different.'

Her mother knelt beside Sister Attracta and stared in front of her, sometimes moving her lips.

'Lord, they want me to give up my baby, Catherine,' Biddy prayed. 'I will never give her up. Sister said to pray for hope. I am hoping to keep her.'

The chapel was cold. Sister Attracta's beads rattled. Biddy's eyes strayed to the brass pots of flowers on the altar, to the carving on the altar railings, the gold tabernacle, and the little red flame above it.

'Our Father who art in heaven, hallowed be thy name,' Sister Attracta began.

Biddy was remembering the rosary at home every night before they went to bed. Her mother's head bowed, body rigid, fingers moving along ebony beads.

'Thy kingdom come. Thy will be done on earth, as it is in heaven.'

'Thy will be done on earth . . . I'll never give Catherine up. Never.'

'Give us this day our daily bread.'

'Give me food for her.'

'And forgive us our trespasses, as we forgive those who trespass against us.'

'I'll never forgive them. Never, never, never.'

'And lead us not into temptation, but deliver us from evil.'

'I'll never deliver her up to them.'

'Amen.'

'I'll find a way.'

13

When her mother had gone, Biddy went to check the laundry list with Nancy. As soon as everything was in order for the deliveries, Nancy said, 'Come up to the ironing-room. I've got a few bits and pieces for the baby.'

There were vests and nappies, a knitted pink dress, and coat and hat to match, in a carrier bag.

Biddy hugged her. 'Where did you get them? They're beautiful.'

'I knitted them and collected the other bits. Listen, Biddy, I have an idea. Sit down.' Nancy lowered her voice.

Biddy sat.

'Was that your mother you were saying good-bye to?'

'Yes.'

'Nice-looking woman.'

'She refuses to let me bring the baby home.'

'That's usually the case.'

'I'll think of something. I'm not staying here.'

'You know the way you're always saying that you want to get out?'

'Yes.'

'You know that the nuns go to vespers around six o'clock, and we all go in for our tea.'

'Yes.'

'Well, supposing I left an empty basket out, and you were to hide in it. You could scarper when no one was looking.'

'How?'

'Easy. I'd leave the big doors ajar, and close them when you'd gone.'

Biddy stood up. 'I couldn't do it. I wouldn't leave Catherine behind.'

'Take her with you! You've got the clothes, and nicking a bottle would be simple enough.'

'How would I get her out of the nursery?'

'Sneak her out while you're feeding her.'

'I couldn't keep her in the laundry basket for long, she'd cry and I'd get caught. What would they do to me then?'

'Get Mother Catherine to bring her down to you as soon as vespers start.' Nancy lit a cigarette, and blew smoke into the air.

Biddy said, 'That's a good idea. Could she carry her all that way?'

'Mother Catherine is shrewd enough to get someone to help her. She'll think of something. I've got girls out in baskets before.'

'Did you?'

'Girls like you, who killed themselves working and deserved a break.'

'What did they say when they found out?'

'There was murder, but the girls were gone. And they never suspected little old me.' Nancy had a glint in her eyes.

'Listen. When the bell rings for vespers, and the coast is clear, you could be off.'

'I could go to Mrs Brophy.'

Nancy dragged on her cigarette. 'You could. You're bright, Biddy. Streets ahead of the others. And I'd love to see their faces when they find out.'

'You're not that fond of them.'

'I hate them.' Nancy laughed. 'Think about it. You could go to your Anthony instead of waiting for him to come to you.'

'I don't know where he is.'

'It's up to you.' Nancy took a bar of chocolate from her overall pocket and broke it in two. 'Think about it.' She gave Biddy half the chocolate.

Two days later Nancy hid Biddy in one of the baskets next to the side door. Biddy crouched down, her head on her knees. There was silence. After a while, the clock struck six and she could hear footsteps as the girls went in to tea. She waited for what seemed ages, her heart hammering in her ribcage. Eventually she heard slow footsteps and the tap–tap of a cane.

'Biddy?'

Biddy lifted the lid of the basket to see Mother Catherine standing there, the baby in the crook of her arm.

'I did it.' Mother Catherine looked delightedly at Biddy as she got out of the basket and took the baby in her arms.

'Thank you,' Biddy whispered.

Nancy appeared soundlessly beside them. 'The coast is clear. Come on, I'll let you out. Here's a bottle and an old coat in case it gets cold. You had better get going.'

There were tears in Nancy's eyes as she watched Biddy hug Mother Catherine.

'God be with you,' the old nun said. 'I'll pray for you both.'

Biddy walked through the thick doors of the convent guarded by Mother Catherine and Nancy. Head erect, she continued down the avenue, eyes on the iron gate, and the road ahead. She wore her new shoes and stockings, and the dress Monica Price had given her. The baby was hidden in the coat Nancy had thrust into her arms.

Rain clouds gathered and the sky was a dull grey. As she approached the gate, it began to rain. Her confidence vanished. Would Mother Dymphna be looking out of the window? Afraid to look over her shoulder, she half-expected to hear footsteps behind her. Where would she tell them she was going? She would babble and say something idiotic.

As soon as she reached the gate, she ran out on to the footpath, skidding on gravel and almost falling. 'Damn, my new shoes,' she swore. Why had she not remembered to scuff the soles before putting them on?

Once she was safely on the main road, she slowed down, put on her coat and covered Catherine with it. Her heart hammered with every step she took. Her pulse throbbed in her neck. They'll murder me if they catch me, she thought, forgetting about her new dress, the shoes, what she looked like. 'Keep going, keep going, there's no stopping now. I can't get caught. It's too dangerous,' she told herself.

She walked down the tree-lined street of redbrick houses in the drizzling rain. The houses were big, newly painted, their long gardens setting them back from the road. The lawns were closely shaved, the hedges neatly clipped.

Purple crocuses raised their tiny battered heads, determined to survive the needles of rain.

Rich people lived in those houses, Biddy thought. People who sent their clothes to the Magdalen Laundry, and served tea in bone china cups.

Traffic thickened. The rain teemed down, bounced off the pavement, and raced along overflowing gutters. Biddy walked quickly, head bowed to dodge wet drops that hit her face like accusing fingers. She waited in the queue at the bus stop. The bells of the church chimed as the bus drew up alongside her, splashing her feet with muddy water.

'I am not frightened. I am not frightened.'

She clambered on to the bus, and moved along quickly to the back. Slowly she sat down and leaned back, letting her breath out. Taking her purse from her pocket, she prayed that the baby hidden inside her coat would continue to sleep, however uneasily, and that hunger pains would not wake her yet.

The other passengers were wet. Water dripped from their clothes and squelched in their shoes. Perhaps they were thinking of home, the fireside and an evening meal. Biddy held her baby's tiny unsuspecting hand. The couple in front leaned towards one another, her face serene, his protective. Lights shone from windows as the bus drove past.

The bus stopped near the Brophys' house. Biddy alighted. The street-lamps mirrored pools of light in puddles, as the moon slid in and out from behind dark clouds. Light shone through the curtains of the Brophys'. Biddy shivered as she rang the bell.

Mrs Brophy opened the door.

'Biddy!' she said in amazement. 'You're the last person I expected to see. Come in. Come in. What are you doing out on a night like this? You wouldn't send a dog out.'

Biddy followed her into the kitchen. Ned was sitting by the fire, legs stretched out, head buried in the newspaper.

'Biddy's here.'

He looked up, startled.

'Hello, Mr Brophy.'

'Biddy. What are you doing here?'

'I've run away.'

'Does Anthony know?'

'No, Mr Brophy. I was hoping you'd get a message to him,' Biddy said.

She opened her coat to reveal the baby.

'Don't you think you should let him know?' Biddy's eyes were bold and proud.

'Oh Biddy—' Mrs Brophy began, stretching out her arms to take the baby.

Mr Brophy stood up, and went to the door. 'I'll get a message to him somehow.' He shuffled down the hall, putting on the light to get his hat and coat.

The door banged shut.

'Are you tired, love? Sit down and warm yourself. What a beautiful baby. What's her name?'

'Catherine. After an old nun I got friendly with.'

'Lovely.'

'Do you know where Anthony is, Mrs B?'

'No, love, I don't. What made you run away?'

'I thought it was time to make my own decisions.'

'Good for you. But what if you can't find Anthony, and what if the baby gets sick?'

'I'll manage. I know all about babies.' Biddy produced a bottle from her coat pocket. 'Could I heat this up, please, before she starts crying?'

'Certainly.'

'It was unbearable, Mrs Brophy, unbearable,' Biddy said as they went into the kitchen.

Mrs Brophy rocked the baby in her arms.

'It's a long time since I held a baby as tiny as this,' she said when Biddy returned with the heated bottle.

The baby cried. Biddy took her and gave her the bottle.

'I don't understand why Anthony didn't come back to the laundry.'

Mrs Brophy shrugged. 'You hear of all sorts of things. He could be held up somewhere.'

'Held up?'

'If I'd known you were coming, I'd have had the bed made up.'

'I'm sorry, Mrs B. I couldn't bear the thought of spending another night in that place. The nuns would have found a home for her any minute. She's entitled to a home with her own parents.'

'You've grown up a lot.'

'You can say that again.'

'Hungry?'

'Starving. I'm always starving.' Biddy laughed.

'I don't expect they treated you so well.'

'I didn't expect to be treated well, but to be treated like an animal . . . Jesus forgave Mary Magdalene. I'll never forgive *them*.'

'How did you survive at all?'

'I had Grace and Nancy and poor old Sister Catherine to help me. Only for that I wouldn't have.'

'Poor love, you were lucky in some ways.'

Mrs Brophy noticed the sunken cheeks, and the sadness in Biddy's smile.

'I'll get you something to eat.'

She went into the kitchen, rummaged in the bread bin, opening and shutting the doors of presses.

'Fresh bread from Enzo's, cheese, chicken, a bit of ham, tomatoes,' she called out.

'Sounds like a feast!'

Mrs Brophy returned and set the table. Her hands cut the bread and buttered it as she waited for the kettle to boil.

'Do you think Mr Brophy knows where Anthony is, Mrs B?'

Mrs Brophy's face was in shadow, so Biddy could not see it.

'I don't think so, love. But he'll do his best to find out. Meanwhile you could do with a bit of fattening.'

Biddy sat at the table and ate, chewing with relish while Mrs Brophy held the baby.

'I haven't tasted bread as good as this since I left Enzo's. How are they?'

'Much the same. Making pots of money. Maureen was asking for you. But of course I had no news for her.'

Biddy ate in silence. Then Mrs Brophy said, 'Don't the nuns make beautiful bread?'

'Not for the likes of us. Maybe for the priests.'

'Did you get anything decent to eat at all?'

'No. The food was awful. Sometimes, when we were so hungry that we couldn't stay standing, we ate out of the bucket of scraps at the back door.'

'My God.'

'That's how I got the sores on my head, I think.'

'Where did you get the courage to run?'

'One of the girls, and the old nun. I didn't want them to give my baby away.'

'They must be at their wits' end.'

'I don't care.' Biddy spoke with her mouth full, as she helped herself to a drumstick.

'How did you escape? Weren't you scared?'

'I hid in an empty laundry basket. I was so excited, I hadn't time to be scared, until I was out the gate. It was like an adventure – something you read about.'

She licked her fingers. 'That was delicious.'

'Was it a difficult birth, Biddy?'

To Mrs Brophy's surprise, Biddy's face went red.

'It wasn't easy. Afterwards I felt good. Sort of cleansed or something. Not afraid any more.' She thought for a minute. 'Responsible. That's what I felt.'

'Where will we put the baby to sleep?'

'We put May in a drawer when Mammy first brought her home from hospital. She was too small for the cot.'

'Good idea.' Mrs Brophy got to her feet. 'Don't worry, love. We'll manage somehow.'

'Thank you, Mrs B. I'm very grateful.'

They went upstairs, and Biddy stood in the half-light of the landing, the baby in her arms, while she waited for Mrs Brophy to prepare the drawer.

'We'll find Anthony too for you. I'm sure we will,' Mrs Brophy said.

Biddy gently rocked the baby. 'I want Anthony to

come for us because he wants us. Not because he feels obliged to.'

'He will.'

Catherine sighed contentedly in her sleep. Mr Brophy did not return, and Biddy went to bed.

The sunlight streaming in the window woke her up. She heard Mrs Brophy moving around downstairs. Catherine stirred in the drawer, her restless movements an indication that she was about to cry.

Biddy dressed quickly and took her downstairs. Ned Brophy was sitting at the table, the morning paper propped against the teapot.

'Good morning.' His eyes did not leave the page.

'Good morning, Mr Brophy.' Biddy waited for him to speak.

Mrs Brophy had a bottle ready for Catherine. 'Sit down and feed her. I'll make the toast.'

'Did you find out anything about Anthony?' Biddy asked Mr Brophy.

'I think so.' Mr Brophy continued reading.

'It's very agitating when a person doesn't answer a question fully,' Mrs Brophy said.

'You don't say much yourself.'

'I talk when I have something to say. You do most of your talking in the pub. So let's hear what you found out.'

He put down the newspaper. 'Anthony's in London. Gone for an interview with the Boxing Control Board.'

After breakfast Biddy went upstairs to change the baby.

'Keep an eye on her,' Ned said to his wife. 'She could be in for a long wait.' He looked peeved.

'I'll watch her like a hawk.'

'I'm serious, Madge.'

'So am I. It's about time someone kept an eye on the poor child. She's been through the mill.'

His response was a grudging nod of the head.

A week went by, but there was still no word of Anthony. Now Biddy allowed herself to see the truth for what it was. Although Anthony had asked her to marry him, she had seen how relieved he was when she had refused. He did not want to be tied down. He would disappear like her mother had said he would. All her plans for herself and Catherine would count for nothing because he had no interest in them. As the truth became obvious, she could not bear the pain. A ray of hope flickered as she watched her sleeping baby. At least she had Catherine, and she was not a prisoner any more. She would take care of her daughter and plan her future. Education would be a priority. Catherine would go to a proper school. Biddy would throw herself into the business of teaching her herself. Take her to visit museums, art galleries and plays. She would make sure she had friends and would entertain them. Catherine would have a nice bedroom, with bright curtains, wallpaper, a desk, a chair, and a dressing-table. In her mind's eye Biddy could hear her daughter's footsteps on the stairs, her light young voice calling to her, her laughter, energy, enthusiasm and eagerness. They would have a wonderful life together. But where? And how would she manage for money?

There and then Biddy resolved to educate herself somehow so that she could become the fashion designer she longed to be. She would make her daughter proud of her yet.

14

Gertie telephoned the bank manager to see how much her savings had amounted to.

'Mr Grimes, we're going to America for Lizzie's wedding, and what with the cost of the fare, and obviously we'd like to bring presents . . . We expect to be away a couple of months.' She was gabbling.

'One thousand, five hundred pounds.'

'One thousand, five hundred pounds,' Gertie repeated, and heard Mr Grimes chuckle down the line.

'Don't sound so surprised. You have been saving consistently since you opened the guest-house. And there's the interest to take into consideration. Of course, with the boost in trade that you can expect in early summer . . .'

Gertie stood in the hall, trying to take in the enormity of her wealth, and almost forgot to thank Mr Grimes and replace the receiver. All that money was the culmination of her own brainwave to turn their home into a business and make money. She was astonished at her own cleverness. When she finally sat down in the kitchen, she realised that she was not so much overwhelmed as grateful. Gertie had

had to save and penny-pinch all her life. She had been grateful to be able to educate her children, and keep her home.

Remembering the hardship of the war years, when Vicky and Lizzie were in boarding school, she wondered how she had managed. The news was full of disasters: battleships were being destroyed, people were terrified. Although Ireland had remained neutral, Gran and Gertie found it difficult to deal with the daily problems of keeping the family warm, fed and dressed. Tea was rationed, and the bread was grey. Oranges and bananas were not to be found.

The days were dreary and there did not seem to be much to look forward to. Sometimes they gave up hope of the war ever ending. Yet they were luckier than the British people, and they realized that. They were able to buy meat and home-grown vegetables, listen to the wireless, and go to the cinema. And they did not have to endure the blackout.

Suddenly the war was over. Europe was freed. Prisoners of war returned home. Gertie had known that the chances of finding Paul were slim. As the months passed, and memories of him faded, Karen came to terms with the fact that she was a widow. All that seemed so long ago.

Now they could pay for the trip to America, and buy some new clothes for Bill and herself. Because Gertie wanted to bring Gran's trunk with Lizzie's trousseau in it, they would travel by ship. The thought of airports and flying did not appeal to her anyway. Karen and Paul enjoyed their trip to visit Paul's parents, and by all accounts John had taken to the transatlantic flight like a duck to water.

The garden was full of bright flowers, and the low branches of lilac and cherry trees were scattering their blooms. Bill had cut the lawn, and was about to plant out the vegetable garden. Gertie and Mrs Keogh had done the spring-cleaning. The lace curtains had been washed and pegged out on the line, and the tablecloths were washed, ironed, and returned to the drawer in the dining-room waiting to be used.

Mrs Keogh had also stripped down and scrubbed the kitchen shelves. She had enjoyed the preparation for the new summer season more than at any time since she had come to work in Santa Maria. She was to take charge of the running of the guest-house while Gertie was away, and would continue as cook and general help, much to her disgust.

'I can't do everything,' she had grumbled when Gertie had given her her list of duties.

'You're needed in the kitchen. Without your cooking we'd have no visitors.'

That bit of praise pacified her temporarily.

'Who'll serve the tables?'

'I was thinking of asking Biddy Plunkett to give us a hand.'

'Biddy Plunkett.' Mrs Keogh went purple. 'Sure she's . . .'

'Now, Mrs Keogh, watch what you're saying.'

'I was only going to say that with the baby and all . . .'

'She's a great little worker, you have to admit.'

'What about the baby?'

'She can bring her along.'

'Gertie Doyle, have your lost your mind? How can she serve tables and mind a baby at the same time?'

'I thought you'd be willing to give her a hand.'

'I never said I wouldn't.'

The house bereft of the Doyles was a silent, strange place. No footsteps or rattling saucepans, no snatches of jingles from 'Hospital Requests', no washing flung carelessly on kitchen chairs, no doors or windows left open.

Gertie and Bill's chairs by the fireplace were empty. There was no clutter in the kitchen, or dirty dishes to wash. John was the one Mrs Keogh missed most. No laughter, no tears or running footsteps, and no spontaneous kisses. She thought that the loneliness would drive her crazy until one day a taxi arrived bringing unexpected guests recommended by friends who had stayed in 'Santa Maria' the previous year. Suddenly the house was filled with noise, laughter, demands for tea, hot-water bottles, extra pillows, morning calls, breakfast.

Mrs Keogh went to the Plunketts' house to get a message to Biddy that her help was urgently needed.

15

When Biddy returned to Dun Laoghaire, everything was different. It was not that people she knew went out of their way to either greet her or ignore her. It was that the kind of anonymity she had hoped for in her imagination was impossible. She could see from the eyes of neighbours that they perceived her as someone with an aura of tragedy surrounding her.

She would always remember the first day back, walking down the street with her pram, nodding to a few people here and there. Their whispers, as she passed by, caught up with her and followed her.

Biddy had given birth out of wedlock – a scandal that she knew would cling to her for the rest of her life. It would be the only thing that she would be remembered for in Dun Laoghaire.

The house was empty, the key under the mat. May's skipping rope was abandoned in the hall; probably put through the letterbox in her haste to be off somewhere. Annie's cardigan was slung across a chair in the kitchen. As she sat in the kitchen listening to the familiar tick of the clock, and the wireless in the corner that was never switched off, Biddy realized that life at home had gone on normally without her. She was the one who had changed irrevocably. The changes were subtle. But sitting there alone in the afternoon sunshine, she wanted to cry for the girl she once had been.

She heard the key in the lock, saw the shock on her mother's face when she came into the kitchen and found her.

'Biddy! You got my message then?'

'Yes.'

'We heard you'd run away. The nuns wrote. I was worried sick until Father Breen told me you were at the Brophys'.' Her face was taut with strain as she looked into the pram.

'Who told Father Breen?'

'Someone called Grace told him she thought you might have gone to the Brophys'. Was he there?' Mrs Plunkett could not bring herself to say Anthony's name.

'No.'

'I could have told you. Are you on your way to "Santa Maria"?'

'Gertie has offered me a room in their basement for Catherine and myself. And plenty of work for the summer. They're booked out.'

'That's only for the summer. You'd have had a better chance with the nuns. They'd have kept you and looked after you for the rest of your life.'

Catherine stirred.

'She's due a feed.' Biddy lifted her out of the pram.

'She's a nice little thing.'

With outstretched arms Mrs Plunkett took the baby, unable to conceal her fascination with her. 'I could mind you the odd evening if your mammy's working. Take you for a walk.'

'That'd be great.' Biddy's eyes lit up. 'But you don't have to.'

'I know I don't have to.' Ita Plunkett's voice was rough. 'I wouldn't mind. That's what I'm saying.'

'Thanks.' Biddy concentrated on feeding Catherine to stop herself from crying.

When she did look at her mother, she saw the defeated look in her face. It was as if Ita Plunkett had finally realized that she had no control over Biddy's life.

Biddy felt like an outsider as dinner was being prepared until her mother said, 'Stay and have a bite with us. It's only stew but there's plenty.'

'Ah, no thanks, I'd better be going.' Embarrassed, Biddy fussed with the pram. 'Anyway, I promised Mrs Doyle I'd be up as soon as I could.'

'You'll have to wait till Annie and May get home. They'll be raging if they miss seeing the baby.'

'All right then. But I can't stay too long.'

Biddy returned to work at 'Santa Maria'. Mrs Keogh helped her to take care of Catherine.

'You're brave, Biddy,' she said to her one day when they were having their tea. 'You managed to keep your baby against all the odds, and hold your head high. I admire you, and I feel ashamed.'

'Ashamed?' Biddy looked at her.

'I'm afraid I wasn't much help to you in your hour of need.'

'Don't worry about it, Mrs Keogh, a lot of people felt the same.'

'But I was worse than that. I never gave Gertie your telephone message, that time you rang from the laundry.'

'You didn't?'

'No, and I feel guilty now. I thought it would be best not to involve Gertie. But I'll do anything I can to make up for it, Biddy. Anything. It's only now I realize how hard it was for you. I thought Anthony would do the decent thing and marry you.'

'Just because he wasn't ready to settle down doesn't make him a bad person, Mrs Keogh. I don't think I want to settle down myself yet. Anyway, I managed didn't I?'

'Yes, and there's great credit due to you for that.' Admiration shone from Mrs Keogh's eyes as she looked at Biddy and then at Catherine.

'I have no regrets about keeping Catherine, and I don't expect it to be an easy road.'

'Any word of Anthony?'

'I had a letter from him. He's back in London training for the boxing championships again, and he's delighted with himself.'

'Some people have all the luck,' Mrs Keogh sniffed.

'I'm delighted for him. It's what he always wanted, and he deserves it.'

'What about the rumours about him being a member of the IRA?'

'That's all they were – rumours.' Biddy did not tell Mrs Keogh that Anthony had written that he had been disillusioned with the IRA and had got out of it before he became seriously involved. Nor did she tell her that Anthony had a new incentive to win the championships – his baby daughter – and that he hoped to return home with a trophy for her that would make her proud of him.

The activity in the guest-house kept her mind occupied, although Anthony was never completely out of it. At night she dreamed about him. Biddy missed Gertie's help and reassurance and found the work hard.

'The Grimshaws are leaving tomorrow. And the Burtons,' Mrs Keogh said.

'Good. I'll be able to rest me feet up a bit.' Biddy sank into a chair, relief written all over her face.

'No you won't. I'm expecting a full house by Sunday night.' Mrs Keogh was full of importance.

'No rest for the wicked.'

'You said it. Now I must go and see if that little babby's all right.' Mrs Keogh darted out to the garden.

The following Sunday was hot. Catherine slept in her pram in the garden, under the shade of the apple tree. The borders were full of coloured dahlias, and roses were bursting with scented blooms; bees rejoiced in their fragrance, and drowsily buzzed around their precious nectar. In the afternoon Mrs Keogh slept on a deckchair, exhausted from the rush of the morning breakfasts. The newspaper shielding her face from the sun rose slightly with each gentle snore. Biddy folded the sheets from the clothes-line into neat piles, ready for the next day's ironing.

Then she spread the old picnic rug on the grass and took Catherine out of her pram to feed her. Catherine drank peacefully, eyes closed, dark lashes sweeping her cheeks, her tiny hand clutching the bottle.

Ita Plunkett arrived and came out to the garden to sit in the shade near Biddy.

She took out her knitting to show Biddy. 'I thought I'd knit a few things for Catherine. You can't have enough clothes for a baby.'

'That's gorgeous.' Biddy held the unfinished dress in her hands to admire the fine shell stitches. 'As soon as I've saved enough, I'm going to buy her some clothes. She's growing out of everything she has.'

'And buy something for yourself. You deserve it.' Ita was looking at Biddy, noticing how much weight she had lost. 'Annie and May are gone down the pier to hear the brass band. The teacher told them that a bit of culture wouldn't do them any harm, and they're getting a composition about the brass band tomorrow. They'll be up to collect me and see Catherine.'

A shadow fell across the lawn. Biddy looked up and saw

the dark shape of a man. Scrambling to her feet, clutching
Catherine, she straightened her dress with her free hand,
then pushed back her hair. PJ from the bakery stood there.

'Hello. What are you doing here? I wasn't expecting
you.'

'I'm sorry I didn't let you know. I took a notion
and came. It wasn't hard to find.' He looked around.
'Nice place.'

'This is my mother.'

'Nice to meet you,' PJ said.

Mrs Plunkett nodded. 'Delighted, I'm sure.'

PJ turned to Biddy.

'You're looking well.'

'I'm not so bad.'

PJ was dressed in a dark grey suit and white shirt. His hair
was slicked back with Brylcreem and his face was shining. 'I
brought something for Catherine, and a few chocolates for
yourself.' He handed Biddy a big brown parcel.

'Thanks, PJ. You shouldn't have.'

'I hope I'm not interrupting anything.'

'You're all right. We're sunbathing. That's all.' Biddy
opened the parcel. It contained a teddy bear with rolling
eyes, and a large box of Cadbury's Dairy Milk.

'It's lovely. Her first toy. You're very kind, PJ. Thanks.'

'It's nothing. I was stuck in town in this heat and I
suddenly thought to myself why don't I go out and see
Biddy and Catherine.' His eyes moved from Biddy to the
baby and then to Ita Plunkett.

Ita Plunkett nodded to PJ, then concentrated on her knitting.

'May I hold her a minute?' PJ held out his arms and Biddy put Catherine into them.

'She's a lovely little one. A bit small.'

Their voices woke up Mrs Keogh.

'Where did you all spring from?' Mrs Keogh scrambled out of her deckchair. 'It's good to see you, Ita. You must think me terrible falling asleep like that.'

'Nonsense. Isn't it your afternoon off?'

'This is PJ from the bakery, Mrs Keogh.'

'Nice to see you.'

Catherine snuggled into PJ. 'Sorry I can't shake hands.' PJ held Catherine closer.

'I'm sure you're all parched. I'll make a cup of tea,' Mrs Keogh said.

'Take off your jacket. You'll be baked otherwise,' said Biddy.

'Baked. That's nothing new to me,' PJ laughed. 'But I could murder a cup of tea.'

Ita Plunkett folded her knitting. 'I'll give you a hand, Mrs Keogh,' she said. They went inside together.

Biddy took Catherine while PJ removed his jacket and sat on the grass.

'It's getting hotter,' he said, opening the top button of his shirt, and rolling up his sleeves.

'How have you been?' Biddy asked, sitting down near him.

189

'Obeying orders, keeping my head down.'

'Sounds like a battle.'

'It is. You know that.'

'Only because you make it difficult for yourself.'

'Who cares. It's a job. And Enzo's looking for an apprentice. I might apply.'

'That'd be great.'

'How about yourself?'

'I'm all right. We're getting busy and the Doyles will be away for another while.'

'I bet you miss them.'

'I do. Gertie says I can stay on after the season. So at least I've somewhere to live. She's been very good to me.'

'She knows the value of you. You're a good worker. Enzo and Maureen talk about you often. They missed you when you left. So did I.'

'I didn't have much choice.'

'I know. Would you like to come to the pictures with me one night, Biddy? *The Toast of New Orleans* is on in the Savoy. Mario Lanza. Supposed to be very good.'

Apprehension and the sun made PJ's face shiny.

'I'd love to. Only as a friend though. I don't want to get . . . involved with anyone.'

'That's all right with me, Biddy. Whatever you say. How about Saturday night?'

'I'll ask Mrs Keogh if it's all right.'

'Great.'

16

Gertie was in Lizzie's kitchen with an apron on over her good frock. She checked the ribs of beef in the oven, and then placed on the table the lace tablecloth that Gran had been making for Lizzie before she died.

The first thing Gertie did when they arrived was to clear away bridal magazines, and swatches of fabric which littered the table. There were pictures of brides and photographs of bridesmaids' dresses, cut out and pasted on cardboard. Articles on wedding etiquette, skin care and advertisements for bridal cars were strewn all over the apartment. The panic in the frenzied preparations for Lizzie's forthcoming wedding was evident in the various choices of discarded material.

Bill refused to comment when Gertie complained about the state of the bedroom that they were expected to sleep in. The room had been taken over by Lizzie's clothes. Her wedding veil flowed out from the head of an old dummy, across the ceiling, and was pinned on the far wall, to keep it from creasing.

When Gertie and Lizzie were alone, Gertie opened

the steamer trunk and lifted the curved lid.

'I loved that trunk when I was a child. Gran always kept it in the corner of her bedroom. She used to let me look inside it as a special treat. I knew everything in it. Hauling it across the Atlantic was no fun, but it was the only way I could think of to pack your trousseau and bring the trunk at the same time.' Gertie lifted out the top tray with its wallpapered section. It was packed with tissue-wrapped treasures. She put it down on the floor.

'You went to a lot of trouble, Mam.'

Lizzie began unwrapping the scented tissue paper that rustled delicately as she examined the soaps, talcum powder, lavender water, lotions, face cloth and sponge, replacing each item carefully in its wrappers. The rest of the trunk was filled with linen sheets, towels, a pink satin dressing gown and silk night-dresses, made by Gertie.

Lizzie reached in and took out Gran's wedding dress, still wrapped in brown paper.

'Gran gave me this a long time ago. We used to look at it together.' Lizzie lifted out yards of lace, and held it against her. It was as light as a sigh.

'No other dress would do you,' Gertie said. 'Gran had a twenty-two inch waist when she wore it.'

'She told me. Often. I've been watching my weight for the last six months.'

Lizzie stood fingering the softness of the fabric. The raised threads brought back memories of Gran and the secrets she had told Lizzie about how women were never properly prepared for the marriage state, and the quirkiness of men. Gran always wore a closed-off expression when she talked about men, and kept her lips pursed as if she hardly trusted herself to speak of such matters.

'Try it on,' Gertie urged.

Lizzie hardly recognized herself or her reflection in the long mirror. The bodice and waist fitted snugly, and the full skirt shifted as she moved. Suddenly marriage represented a much more serious consequence than an occasion for festivities. It was good-bye to carefree days, dances with the girls, trips to the cinema on a whim, midnight forages to the drugstore. Gran's wedding dress represented responsibilities, a home of her own, children.

'You look magnificent.' Gertie's admiration shone in her eyes.

As Gertie set out the silver knives and forks she had brought from Ireland and put dishes on a warming plate, she thought how Gran would have loved to have seen Lizzie getting married in her dress. And she would have made a proper three-tiered rich fruit wedding cake; those American sponge cakes didn't look right at all. Gertie hoped Lizzie would be home from work on time.

Her daughter's head was in the clouds at the moment, so she could not be relied upon to remember anything. In fact, she wondered if it had been a good idea to keep this party a surprise. And where was Bill? He had promised to be back in time to help her. No doubt Uncle Mike was regaling him with stories in The Blarney Stone pub in Queens. Still, it was a relief to know that Vicky had arrived safely from Canada, and would be there shortly. Gertie was looking forward to having her family together again. She was tired after the long journey, but it was worth it.

The doorbell rang. Uncle Mike's bulk obliterated the light in the hall as Gertie opened the door. He was followed by Bill.

'A sound place, Gertie. Plenty of pubs. I could get used to living here.'

'I'm glad you're back. Come and see my handiwork.'

They followed her into the dining-room.

Bill put his arm around her. 'You've done a great job.'

Gertie took him to one side. 'Don't give Mike any more to drink,' she whispered, then in a loud voice said to both of them, 'Are you going to stand there all evening, or will you give me a hand?'

Uncle Mike surveyed the salmon on a silver platter, decorated with cucumber and lettuce leaves.

'Isn't that grand,' he said. 'It looks as if it leaped out of the river on to the plate.'

'You can help by moving the chairs into the dining-room, and Bill, you can polish those wine glasses.' She looked anxiously at her watch. 'I hope the beef will be cooked in time. How will we fit everyone at the table?'

'Stop fussing. We'll manage.' Mike began taking chairs out of the kitchen.

'Have a drink, woman, and relax. Everything will be all right.' Bill handed her a glass of sherry.

Gertie removed her apron, smoothed her hair, and sat down to sip her sherry.

It was later than Lizzie had intended when she reached home. She let herself in. Hearing the sound of muffled voices made her hesitate for a moment. When she opened the door of the living-room she gasped with shock. Everyone she ever knew seemed to be there looking at her. Bill, watching her, laughed. Gertie came to enfold her in her arms.

'I wasn't expecting this.' Lizzie hugged her mother.

The room was warm and welcoming with people.

'Your mother has been busy,' Bill said. 'Come and have a look.' Lizzie followed him into the dining-room.

'Oh Mam, the table looks beautiful.' Lizzie gave her mother a hug. 'Thanks for everything, Mam.'

'I hope you'll be happy, that's all.'

'Thank you.' Lizzie kissed her.

'Time for a drink,' Bill announced as Aunt Peggy, Uncle Mike's wife, Sissy, Vicky's mother, and Hermy, Vicky's father, came forward to embrace Lizzie.

'This is a great occasion, Lizzie,' Uncle Hermy said. He was old and stooped, but his eyes twinkled with mischief as he said, 'If your grandmother were here I'd enjoy teasing her.'

'You drove her mad, Uncle Hermy.'

'She took life too seriously. And I don't think she trusted me.'

'She hadn't much reason to,' Auntie Sissy said. 'Not after the way you treated me.'

'It was all in good fun, Sissy. All in good fun.'

'Let's hope Pete Scanlon treats you better.' Sissy raised her glass to Lizzie.

'He will if he knows what's good for him,' Gertie laughed, and Bill said, 'Lizzie's well able to take care of herself.'

There was a loud knock on the door. Olive stood there, Karen, Paul and John behind her. John ran to greet Bill.

'Good to see you.' Gertie hugged them all in turn. 'It seems ages since you left. How are you, Karen? You've put on some weight.'

'Only a little; and we've been having a wonderful time.' Karen's eyes sparkled. 'Haven't we, Paul?'

'Sure have,' Paul beamed.

'How about you, John?' Bill asked. 'Did you go fishing?'

'Yep. I caught the biggest fish.'

Olive sailed into the room, her satin coat shining in the light, her hair tucked into a cocktail hat which was held up with a tortoise-shell comb. She greeted Gertie first, then reached up for a kiss from Bill. Everybody gathered around her and she kissed them all in turn.

'Gertie, I want you and Bill to come back with us for a vacation. We want you to see our ranch in North Carolina.

Paul has been working hard on the farm, and exercising the horses.'

'Wonderful. We'd love to see it all. But—'

'Then it's all arranged. No buts.'

Pete Scanlon arrived wearing the new Donegal tweed jacket Gertie and Bill had brought him. He was followed by his brother Jimmy, whose obvious anxiety at meeting so many people all at once dissolved as soon as he saw Lizzie.

'You look beautiful.' Pete proudly took Lizzie in his arms and kissed her in the middle of the room, to the satisfaction of all the onlookers.

'Shall we eat?' Gertie asked. 'Everything's ready.'

Lizzie was given the place of honour at the head of the table. Bill took Olive's arm and led her to her seat. Karen and Paul followed. John sat on a cushion between them. The doorbell rang again and the girls who shared the apartment with Lizzie were there with colleagues from the hospital. They came in, filling the rooms with more noise and laughter.

When the party was in full swing, Vicky arrived. Resplendent in a low-cut black dress, skirts rustling, head aloft, her neck encased in creamy pearls, she stood in the doorway surveying the guests. They all stopped eating.

'I'm sorry I'm late. I got caught up in the traffic.' She glided across the room, her arms held out to Gertie.

Gertie put down a serving dish to greet her. 'You're here. That's all that matters.'

Lizzie thought how confident and secure Vicky seemed.

'You should have left home earlier,' Sissy said, rising to kiss her daughter.

Vicky turned to smile at her. 'It was unavoidable, I assure you, Mother.'

She went to Lizzie. 'Darling, it's wonderful to see you.'

'You too.'

Conversation resumed. The noise level rose. Gertie served Vicky, then collected dirty dishes as Bill replenished glasses. Vicky, watching Lizzie and thinking of her desire to become Pete Scanlon's wife, wondered how she herself would cope with the loss of her freedom.

Bill got to his feet. 'I would like to thank you all for coming, my dear family and friends, to help us celebrate Lizzie's wedding.'

Expanding his arms to embrace them all, he named each one. 'Now let us drink a toast to the happy couple.'

Everyone rose.

Next morning Vicky lay in bed in Lizzie's apartment, covered only by a single sheet. The apartment, over a grocery store, was close to a subway line. Trains shunted and shuddered throughout the night. Trucks rumbled along alleyways, and old water pipes knocked and groaned. The apartment itself was neat and clean. Floors had been stripped, sanded, stained and polished. Pete had painted the ceilings and walls white, which gave a bright, airy feeling to what was a dingy place when they had first inspected the old linoleum and grey walls. Now it was ready for

Pete and Lizzie to move into once they were married. Meanwhile Lizzie's friend and colleague, Irene, was sharing with her to help with the expenses.

'It was a dubious area once,' Lizzie had explained to Vicky. 'But it has come up in the world what with lawyers and doctors moving in, and it's close to the hospital.'

'I want to see Manhattan,' Vicky said, remembering the drive in from the airport in the taxi the previous day.

She had been overwhelmed by the sight of skyscrapers, apartments and city-centre shops in their glitz and awnings. How was she to know that behind the prosperity and ostentation, the city seethed with street after street of garbage and muggings? That was something that was not immediately obvious to a passing tourist in a taxi.

Lizzie did not make her any the wiser because she loved New York too much to degrade it: the Irishness of Queens, traffic that brought everything to a standstill, and the excitement of downtown New York.

Vicky got up feeling drowsy and searched for coffee in the kitchen. She made herself a cup, and stood at the window looking accusingly at the train track surfacing above the ground, which she held responsible for her broken sleep. Below that pedestrians appeared small against a backdrop of tall buildings: hardware stores, diners, bars, small clothing shops, furniture shops, fruit stands, and book shops.

In the bathroom she squinted into the mirror to inspect her face in the morning sunlight, then washed and dressed quickly in a white blouse with a Peter Pan collar and cotton skirt. In the sterility of the hospital in Canada she usually wore cashmere twin-sets, with tweed skirts, underneath her white doctor's coat.

Lizzie woke up, put on her dressing-gown and came to join Vicky in the kitchen.

'Did you remember to bring your photograph album?' she asked.

'Yes, I'll get it.'

Over breakfast they exchanged photograph albums.

'Do you remember?' Lizzie pointed to the thick, dark pages that held snapshots of happy groups, their smiles covered by the white tissue that preserved the photographs.

'Me when I was a year old. Wasn't I a beautiful baby?'

As Vicky looked, she sensed Lizzie's recollections forming the fragile web that bound them to the past.

Among them were pictures of Lizzie in her christening robe of lace, Gertie proudly holding her up towards the camera; Lizzie as a toddler, her small hand holding Gran's, Gran wearing a dress trimmed with bands of ribbon, gazing at the camera from beneath the brim of her hat, her face serious.

'1939' was marked on the cover of another album of pictures, taken when Vicky came to stay with them. The little bridge outside the back door in Victoria Terrace provided the backdrop for Vicky and Lizzie to pose on their own, or with groups. They wore sun-dresses and hugged one another, or laughed uproariously to the camera.

There were photographs of them in deckchairs, waving arms and legs, and boys in open-necked shirts and corduroy trousers, leaning over them.

Vicky's album contained a photograph of her draped over a deckchair in a sun-dress made by Gran. Another of her wrestling at the beach with Jimmy Scanlon, her dress tucked into her knickers. There were more photographs of them dressed for parties, and a section marked 'Boarding School', with the girls cheering at hockey matches, or singing in choirs, their mouths openly laughing in delight.

There were photographs of Pete Scanlon's car; one of Pete squeezed into the car, waving. Lizzie and Vicky at a fancy-dress party, faces blackened with boot polish. Vicky with Pete Scanlon, her face turned to him. Vicky holding Pete's hand, standing beside him, solemn and adoring. Pete swinging her on a swing, her face suffused with happiness. Lizzie went back to that photograph again.

'Where was this taken?'

'In London. That time I followed him over.'

'You look as if you adored him.'

Vicky laughed. 'Most of the time I was fit to kill him. He didn't want me there, Lizzie. You remember that.'

'That's what you said at the time.'

'Come on, Lizzie, you remember well the way things were. I only wanted him because you were crazy about him. And then he went off and joined the army. It was such a miserable time, what with boarding school looming, and Mum stuck in England in the war. So I ran away. More of a challenge than a dream. Mother didn't want me there and neither did he.'

'And?'

'And what?'

'What happened then?'

'You know well what happened then. I was sent back to Gran and the rest of you. We were all too young, that was the problem.'

Lizzie felt disappointed. She knew that Vicky could have told her more.

'Do you remember playing on the swings and slides?'

They were remembering the time when their rivalry had turned their friendship into a hateful knot of lies, insults and rows. That was when Vicky had become friendly with Sylvia Summers, only daughter of Patrick Summers, Solicitor. She lived in the big house on the corner, and was rich. It was not long before Vicky got herself invited to Sylvia's house.

'Come to tea next Saturday. My mother will telephone to arrange it,' Sylvia had said.

A telephone call was made a week in advance by Sylvia's mother to Gertie. The exact time was stated.

Gran said at the time, 'Stuff and nonsense. It's the likes of them have plenty of time on their hands. Servants to do their dirty work.'

Vicky was popular and had plenty of friends, but because Sylvia was a bit of a mystery, she cultivated her friendship all the more. Gran was anxious about her going. The Summers were known to be reclusive and odd.

Vicky arrived at the house to receive a hearty greeting from Mrs Summers.

'I've been asking Sylvia to bring home a young friend for ages.'

'I'd have come before if you'd invited me,' Vicky said and Sylvia blushed.

Tea was laid on a table in the conservatory: a white cloth, blue china, cakes of all varieties, bowls of fruit, dates, figs, pies and tarts. Vicky, confidence soaring in her new-found friendship, ate heartily, while telling Sylvia's mother that she and Sylvia were best friends at school, even though she, Vicky, was the cleverer.

'Oh, really,' was all Mrs Summers said, her blue eyes watching Vicky lick her fingers as she finished the last morsel of strawberry cream sponge.

Sylvia remained silent, leaving Vicky to do the talking.

When Mrs Summers left the room, Vicky said, 'What's wrong with you?'

'I'm bored,' Sylvia said quietly. 'Let's go out to the garden. I have a hide-out I want to show you.'

'Wow. I love hide-outs.'

'Stop eating then and come on.'

It was a beautiful day. Sylvia led the way through a gate in the walled garden, into a wilderness, where they had to edge their way along a narrow path, overgrown with bracken and brambles. Finally, legs scratched, dresses snagged, they reached a shed half-hidden among old trees. Its back was tucked into a high boundary hedge that divided the Summers' garden from the golf course, and blocked off the strong afternoon sun. Vicky peered through the grimy windows and examined the closed door, its paint dry and peeling.

'A summer house,' Syliva said, opening the big lock with a key she took from under a nearby stone. The door creaked open and Sylvia called out, 'Be careful. The floorboards are rotten.'

The inside was a surprise. The wooden floor was polished, and cane chairs were placed around a small table. Books and magazines lay scattered on it and there was an old trunk in a corner, its brass clasps gleaming. Beside it was a record player.

'Looks as if someone lives here,' Vicky said, sitting on one of the chairs.

'I do.'

Vicky looked at her in amazement.

Sylvia blushed. 'That is sometimes . . . when I want to be alone.'

'Wouldn't mind a place like this myself.' Vicky opened presses and examined their contents.

'Look.' Sylvia opened the trunk. 'These belonged to my mother.' She pulled out old hats, feather boas, long satin dresses, fur stoles, all smelling of must.

'I've got make-up too.' Her face was flushed with excitement. 'Let's get dressed up.'

Vicky took off her dress and put on an ancient cream silk one, then sat good-humouredly, eyes closed, while Sylvia painted her face in bright colours. Looking at her reflection in the cracked mirror of Sylvia's compact, she thought her eyes were too bright, and her cheeks too flushed.

'You can be Katharine Hepburn in *The African Queen*. I'll be Elizabeth Taylor.' Sylvia was so absorbed in unravelling a black velvet dress that she did not see the look of disgust on Vicky's face.

'I'd rather be Elizabeth Taylor,' Vicky began, but Sylvia was not listening. She was putting on the velvet dress.

'What do you think?'

'Gorgeous.' Vicky smiled at her, but Sylvia suddenly said, 'I've changed my mind. Let's pretend we're going somewhere grand. A ball. Put this one on. I'll wear the blue taffeta silk.' She handed Vicky a white silk ball gown, and changed into the blue taffeta, then slipped her feet into a pair of high-heeled shoes. Eagerly she turned to Vicky for her inspection.

'Lovely,' Vicky said, but thought she looked hideous in the old faded dress that smelled musty, and was not very clean.

'You don't think it's quite Elizabeth Taylor. I can tell by the look on you face.'

'No.' Vicky plonked herself in a chair and waited while Sylvia delved deeper into the trunk, dragging out more chiffon and lace. Then she took a record from a neat pile and carefully placed it on the gramophone, then wound it up. Hoagie Carmichael's voice singing 'In the cool cool cool of the evening' filled the little room.

They danced, inventing the steps as they went along.

'I wish you were a boy,' Sylvia said as she grabbed Vicky around the waist and twirled her around.

'Thanks a lot.' Vicky flounced off and sat down until the music stopped.

For a while they paraded around in their dresses, and pretended to drink wine from dirty glasses that Sylvia kept in a cupboard full of junk. Vicky put her hair up. She let Sylvia gather her wide skirt around her waist with a belt. Finally she said, 'Let's do something else. We could explore the garden.'

'Out of bounds,' Sylvia retorted. 'Daddy collects valuable shrubs.'

'Oh well, it's getting late anyway. I'd better be going.' By now Vicky was desperate to get out into the last of the sunshine.

'There's plenty of time.' Sylvia screwed her face up into a scowl.

'I have to go. Gran said not to overstay my welcome.'

Vicky searched for her frock among the jumble of clothes that tumbled out of the trunk. 'Where is it?' she turned to Sylvia. 'Where's my frock?'

'Hidden.' Sylvia pursed her lips as she closed the lid of the trunk and fastened the brass clasps.

'Sylvia, my dress.' Vicky's voice rose. She moved towards Sylvia.

'Careful.' Sylvia stepped backwards, and with one leap was at the door. Vicky saw the key in her hand as she opened it. She went to run after her, but stumbled and tripped on the material of her dress.

'The floorboards are dangerous,' Sylvia shouted as she pulled the door after her. 'You'll break your legs if you fall through them.'

The key turned in the lock. Then Sylvia's face appeared at the window, distorted and ugly in the dirty glass.

'Serves you right, Victoria Clever Clogs Rosenblum,' she called through the window. 'You can yell your stupid head off, but nobody'll hear you.'

Laughing, she disappeared into the thicket.

Vicky craned her neck at the window and caught a glimpse of the sun behind the trees. Soon it would disappear. What would happen when it grew dark and cold? She would freeze to death if she did not die of fright first. Shivering, she resumed her search for her dress, and found it at the bottom of the trunk.

She had known that Sylvia was different, had admired her distant composure, mistaking it for snobbery. Now she realized that Sylvia was mad. Only a mad person would entertain a friend by locking her in a dark and squalid shed. And that laugh of Sylvia's. It was a crazy, theatrical laugh.

Perhaps she had invited friends before and buried them beneath the floorboards.

Vicky waited, and when Sylvia didn't come back, banged

on the door. The gardener must have been passing by. He heard her, and let her out just as Sylvia was slinking up the side of the shed. Vicky pretended not to see her and ran off home without thanking her mother.

'That's an incredible story,' Lizzie said when she had finished. 'I wonder what the gardener thought?'

'He was old and doddery. I could hear them both laughing as I ran. He was probably in on the prank. I got my own back though.'

'How?'

'One day when I was coming up the road I saw her standing on the corner, opposite her house, surrounded by a group of boys. She was animated and preening in her red wool coat. "We've only just moved here," she was saying. One of the boys asked if she would be going to the pictures on Saturday and she said, "I always go to the pictures on Saturdays. Doesn't everyone?" in that high-pitched la-di-da voice. I called out, "Hello, Sylvia" and she ignored me. I shouted, "Hello, boy-crazy," and I shouted "Yes you are. That's all you talk about. Boys and film stars."' She followed me up the street. Her face was thunderous and the boys were laughing at us.

"You apologise," she shouted.

"Make me?" I invited politely.

'"You think you're so smart." She took her pencil-case out of her bag and flung it at me. Luckily it missed my face but hit me on the shoulder. The boys laughed and cheered.

One of them shouted, "Good on you, Sylvia." Another one said, "Let her have it, Vicky." '

'I hope you did.'

'She ran across the road to the safety of her big gates. Once inside she started chanting "Catch me if you can, I'm the gingerbread man." I was furious and chased her into her garden. I remember throwing my school bag at her.'

'Oh Lord.'

'The books spilled out all over her stupid head, and she started bawling, "Leave me alone. I'll tell my daddy on you." ' Then she slouched off up her avenue.

' "See if care, fancy pants," I roared at the top of my voice, while I picked up my books, but I was getting a bit scared.

'She stopped and said, "Who are you calling fancy pants to?" She was hurt. I looked around. "Do you see anyone else around that fits that description? And your house is stupid-looking too." There were visitors there that day. They came out frowning and she fell into her mother's arms. Her mother shook her fist at me, and began to walk towards me. I didn't wait to hear what she was saying. I turned and ran all the way home.'

They remembered the trudge home from school every day. Any diversion was a welcome one, especially if it involved boys. They always walked slower past the boys' school, pausing every now and then to see if anyone was coming out of the gates. When the boys would finally emerge, they would race off without noticing, their minds on some impending football game, or their dinners. A few straggling ones would talk among themselves, or keep their slippery eyes downcast.

'What was Sylvia's secret?' Lizzie mused. 'What did she have that we didn't? The boys liked her, you know.'

'They certainly did. And I was jealous.'

'Why was it so important that boys should like us anyway?'

'So that we could like ourselves. We were in love with the idea of love. Discovering ourselves. Suddenly we knew we could make an impression on others, whether it be with a new bow, or a hairdo, or a new dress. We began to like boys, admire them, cultivate them; find out what interested them.'

'What did interest them?'

'Us. Only they were too shrewd to let us know it.'

'I thought Sylvia had everything. Now I realize that she was a lonely, attention-seeking child.'

'Weren't we all?'

'Some of us more than others.'

17

The city was hot. Apart from the noise, the combined smells of fumes and melting tar were sickening. They were glad to leave the stale air of the stuffy apartment, and take the subway from Queens. Near Queensboro's ornate metal bridge, the city's remarkable skyline was visible. The sun searing through the tops of tall buildings hit rock and steel with its bright blaze. Below, business was transacted in shade, before the subway ran underground to Grand Central Station, obliterating their view.

Bloomingdales was resplendent. In the Food Hall on the ground floor there were aisles of fancy cookies, chocolates of all kinds, rare gourmet food in tins, ice-cream, European delicacies, and varieties of meats and cheeses.

Vicky and Lizzie moved along the aisles inspecting clothes, trinkets, and jewellery. The shoe-repair service reminded them of their childhood shoes: new brown sandals in summer, brown sensible shoes in winter, and thin white runners for gym in boarding school.

Jauntily they took the escalator up to the first floor, where the air was heavy with the overpowering scent of the perfumery. At the cosmetics counter they bought new shades of lipstick, and matching nail polish, then went to purchase underwear. Vicky caught sight of a rail of Italian silk scarves, and found their delicate hand-painted colours irresistible. She bought one for herself and one for Lizzie.

They made their way out of the store and crossed Park Avenue with its elegant apartments, each one attended by a doorman. The distance of another street brought them to Manhattan's more fashionable boutiques, with their glass facades, and gleaming chrome interiors. Designer dresses were displayed in windows on plastic mannequins, together with expensive hand-knits.

On the corner of Central Park South and Fifth Avenue stood the Plaza Hotel. Flags fluttered from the top of the imposing building. Brass glinted in the sunshine. Doormen rushed around the marble and glass entrance hailing taxis, carrying luggage, ordering horse-drawn carriages from the line at the curbside.

'Wow, it's breathtaking.' Vicky stepped back to admire it.

'It looks like a palace.'

'Let's go inside.'

'It's outrageously expensive.' Lizzie was suddenly intimidated by its opulence. 'Famous for its cheesecake though.'

'Come on. We'll have this treat on Hermy, just for old times' sake.' There was a wicked gleam in Vicky's eye that made Lizzie burst out laughing.

They found the café, which was separated from the foyer

by marble pillars. Banquettes of exotic flowers lined the walls, and silver sparkled on cream tablecloths.

'Doesn't it look inviting?'

'I want to be able to fit into my wedding dress,' Lizzie moaned as her eyes lit on the cakes and ices being served.

'Come on. You'll be married long enough.'

'You make it sound like a prison sentence.'

'I imagine it is.' Vicky led the way. 'You might as well enjoy yourself while you can.'

French waiters in black trousers, white shirts and waistcoats hovered in the background. One young man came forward to show them to a table, where a long menu awaited their inspection.

'It all looks so delicious, I don't know what to choose.' Vicky turned to the waiter for help.

'Everything is magnificent.' He kissed his fingers. 'Like you beautiful ladies.'

Lizzie ordered cheesecake for both of them, anticipating the pleasure of tasting it as they waited.

When the waiter returned with confections on porcelain plates, and two cups of coffee, Lizzie's eyes widened. 'Yummy. I haven't had a treat like this since we went to McDonald's Ice Cream Parlour for our confirmation.'

Vicky nodded, slowly savouring the forbiddingly delicious mouthfuls. 'We spent all our money there.'

'Gran was raging that day.'

'Her fury had more to do with Mrs Keogh than us.'

Vicky and Lizzie were twelve when they made their

confirmation. They had sat at the table in white muslin dresses and veils. They were the focus of attention. Gertie sat to the right of Lizzie, Gran to the left of Vicky. Mrs Keogh cut into the chocolate cake that Gran had baked for the celebration, and took the largest slice for herself. Gran said disparagingly, 'People complain about putting on weight, as if it's someone else's fault.'

Gran had an unnerving habit of starting in the middle of a sentence. 'I wouldn't mind if people were hungry or needed it, but when people are downright fat, chocolate cake is the last thing they need.'

Mrs Keogh continued eating without comment, her face red. Vicky and Lizzie sat there, Vicky drumming her fingers on the table, Lizzie looking at her plate, to avoid Mrs Keogh's embarrassment.

'I bet you girls feel different now that you have been enlightened by the Holy Spirit,' Gertie said to divert Gran, knowing that when she found some offence to sound off about, she would continue relentlessly until everybody was thoroughly irritated, embarrassed or depressed.

'I suppose it's my own fault for making cakes so appetising. It's all right for me. A poor old woman with nothing better to do than to make fancy cakes. Who needs that much cake anyway?'

'I don't.' Vicky stood up.

At this stage she had had enough of being on her best behaviour for this family occasion. Her new gifts from the

Holy Ghost, knowledge, piety and the fear of the Lord, had not helped her to understand adults' behaviour any better. If anything, they made her feel rebellious.

Bill and Gertie tried not to look at Gran, or call on her to enquire or respond to anything. They knew that when she was in a particularly insulting mood, she would not stop until she had caused an angry scene.

Vicky asked for permission to leave the table. Lizzie stood up as soon as she was gone, inventing an excuse to leave too. In their bedroom Vicky removed her dress with a sigh of relief. Her body was not all bones and angles any more, but curves and roundness, and she stood admiring her reflection for a moment. Lizzie came in and threw herself on the bed.

'I hate special occasions, and new scratchy tight dresses. All that "best behaviour" stuff grown-ups preach, with their "dos" and "don'ts" and "maybes".'

'They're the ones who don't know how to behave. Gran's intent on causing trouble.'

'Thinks she's Santa Claus because she made us a cake. Should have iced a sign on it: "Private Property".'

'Let's do something.'

'What?' Vicky asked in a bored voice.

'Let's sneak off to the park.'

On Saturdays and Sundays they played on the swings and slides in the park. On their way there they met May Tully, Tess Matthews and Pauline Byrne returning home from the cinema, still wearing their confirmation veils.

'We're going to McDonald's Ice Cream Parlour,' May informed them. 'Want to come?'

In McDonald's they treated themselves to soda creams, ice-cream cones, and whatever they fancied with their confirmation money. Eventually, when their glasses were licked clean, Pauline Byrne said, 'I feel sick.'

'But you said you'd give me a new hairstyle,' May grumbled.

'She's hoping to get an apprenticeship in Scissors in York Road,' Tess said.

'Come on then. We'll go to my house. Want to come?' Pauline asked everyone. They sat around in Pauline's bedroom watching her twist pipe cleaners into May's hair.

'I'd like a hairstyle like Deborah Kerr's,' Vicky said.

'Your hair is too long.' Pauline took more curlers out of a tin.

'What was the picture you saw about?' Lizzie asked.

'It's about this thief who's wanted by the cops. Up for murder, so he's on the run. Guess how he gets caught?' May looked from one to the other, her eyes dancing.

'How?'

'He robs a bank: buys his sweetheart expensive presents, takes her on a cruise. And guess who's on the cruise?'

'Who?'

'The head of MI5. And his wife gets talking to the sweetheart.'

May's eyes had a faraway, melting look as she recalled the

sweetheart's short bobbed hair, and low-cut dresses. 'I want to look like her.'

'Fat chance of that,' Vicky sneered. 'Betty Hutton in *Annie Get Your Gun* is more your line.'

Vicky began singing 'There's No Business Like Show Business'. Everyone joined in except May.

'Shut up, or I'll break your jaw.' She was furious.

'Did you see *King Solomon's Mines*? Pauline asked.

'Yes,' May piped up. 'Saw it in the Savoy in Dublin. Frightening it was with all those strange animals, reptiles, and birds – beautiful scenery though.'

Vicky turned to Lizzie. 'Come on. We're going home.'

They met Mrs Keogh on the way. She had a face on her that would stop a clock and was complaining about Gran being an old battle-axe.

'You think I should be more appreciative of my good fortune to have a job in your home, clean your dirt, do your washing, and accept your generosity. Let me tell you something, Vicky Rosenblum: I've sacrificed taking care of my own hearth and home to come here and do for you.'

'Oh, Mrs Keogh, I didn't know you cared,' Vicky said.

'Buzz off you little devil. Gertie's right to send the pair of you to boarding school. 'Course the Dominican Convent wouldn't be good enough for the likes of you.'

They walked slowly through Central Park admiring statues, fountains and flower-beds. When they grew tired, the jutting rocks made a cushion for their aching backs. Vicky spread her jacket on the stone and lay back.

The sun got stronger. Lizzie folded her cardigan and used it for a pillow. 'Isn't it lovely here?' she said, looking at the skyscrapers.

Vicky's eyes were closed. 'Reminds me of summers in Ireland. We wore cotton dresses and sat in the grass like this, making daisy chains.'

'I used to thread them through your hair. It was as thick as May Tully's skipping rope.'

'Where did she get that marvellous rope? It was the longest skipping rope I've ever seen, and she was so mean about sharing it.'

'She could skip though. I can still see her wiggling that bum of hers and singing, "Tilly on the telephone, miss a loop you're out."'

'She never missed a loop.'

'And she could turn around, touch the ground, show her shoe, without tripping.'

'Who invented those silly rhymes anyway? I preferred playing ball against the side wall of the basement, and clapping my hands before catching it. Or twirling around.'

'You were the expert.'

The day before the wedding, as his special treat, Uncle Hermy took Vicky and Lizzie by taxi to Elizabeth Arden's.

'Get your hair done, have a facial. You'll love it.' He pressed a wad of notes into Vicky's hand.

'What will you do?' Vicky asked.

'I have some business to attend to.'

'I might have known.' Vicky threw her eyes up to heaven.

Uncle Hermy dropped Lizzie and Vicky at Elizabeth Arden's Beauty Salon, a tall narrow townhouse with a red door located on Fifth Avenue at 54th Street.

The elevator took them up past the fashion boutique on the second floor, past an exercise department and a floor for Swedish massage and paraffin packs, past the facial floor to the hair salon on the twelfth floor. As they got off the elevator, they went straight to the desk.

A petite woman in a white coat came to meet them.

'Hello, my name is Miss Maggie. I'll take your dresses.'

She led them to the changing-rooms at the side of the waiting area and hung up their dresses, handing them gowns to put on.

Lizzie laughed when she saw Vicky in the frilly pink gown and matching carpet slippers. 'You look daft!' she said.

'Speak for yourself,' Vicky replied. 'I feel like a queen.'

After a trim, shampoo and set they were placed under the dryers. Delicate sandwiches were served by a lady carrying a huge wicker basket. They munched happily in sunlight which streamed in through tall windows all around. After their hair was dried, they were taken down to the eleventh floor for a facial. While they reclined, Miss Maya, who specialized in facials, cleansed and toned their skin, while their fingers and feet were soaked in scented water, massaged, manicured and polished. While their polish dried to a brilliant finish, their make-up was applied. Then they were escorted back to the hair salon for the final comb-out.

Enthralled, they sat staring at themselves in the mirrors.

'Hermy won't recognize us.' Lizzie shook her head to admire her shimmering curls.

'I'd love to see May Tully's face now,' Vicky said, her eyes riveted on the reflection of her page-boy's bob.

18

When Gertie came into Lizzie's bedroom on the morning of her wedding, she was lying in her bed staring at the ceiling.

'What is it, Lizzie? Having second thoughts?' She sat on the side of the bed.

Lizzie looked at her and smiled, unable to express her feelings of bewilderment, joy, wonder and nervousness. Longing for her mother's comfort she sat up in bed and put out her arms.

Gertie hugged her.

'Be sure and let me know if anything goes wrong, Lizzie.'

'What could possibly go wrong? This is what I've always wanted.' Lizzie seemed surprised at her mother's undue concern.

Her mother shivered. 'Pete Scanlon worries me.'

'You shouldn't say such a thing. And at a time like this!' Bill said, coming into the room.

'Now's as good a time as any,' Gertie retorted.

'Pete's wonderful.' Lizzie's face glowed as she spoke.

★   ★   ★

Elizabeth Mary Doyle married Peter James Scanlon in St Patrick's Church, Queens, New York, at eleven o'clock on the morning of June 4th, 1951.

The church was perfumed with the blooms of flowers. Sheaves of lilies adorned the altar. Garlands of gold and white roses wreathed the altar rails, their perfume mingling with the scent of candle-grease and incense. Gertie and Olive sat in the front row, on either side, their faces half-hidden by the wide brims of their hats. Everyone turned towards the church door as the organ fanfare announced the entrance of the bride.

Gertie gasped at the beauty of her own daughter, as, weighted down in antique lace, a bouquet of marguerites in her hand, she began the slow journey down the aisle on Bill's arm.

Vicky, her bridesmaid, held her head high above the coral blue rucks of her satin dress, while another friend, Irene, walked beside her, each holding an end of the long train. As they walked slowly to the altar rails, where Pete stood waiting with Jimmy, his best man, Vicky was reminded of their childhood: of how they practised being ladies, strutting around in long, tight-waisted gowns, given to them by Dr Pearson. Remembering Pete in those days she thought of the laughing, wild boy, with blond hair and a smattering of freckles across his nose, playing games on the street. He was forever pretending to be aloof.

Standing there in his wedding suit, with his hair slicked back, he seemed dazed and vulnerable.

They knelt before the altar as the Mendelssohn ended. Vicky turned back Lizzie's veil over the crown of daisies that held her hair in place, and with Irene's help arranged the bridal train for the ceremony. Lizzie smiled reassuringly at Pete, who looked surprised and mesmerized by it all. He took her hand and squeezed it reassuringly as Monsignor Cleary, wearing green and cream vestments, began the Mass.

When it was time to take their vows Monsignor Cleary turned to face the bridal couple. 'Do you Elizabeth Mary Doyle take Peter James Scanlon to be your lawful wedded husband?' The voice of the monsignor boomed into the silence.

'I do.'

'Peter James Scanlon, do you take Elizabeth Mary Doyle to be your lawful wedded wife?'

'I do.'

As the bride and groom entered the vestry for the signing of the register, the organ played. Music soared high up above the stained-glass windows into the eaves, straining, reaching, and ending in a fanfare of chords. When they re-emerged, with Lizzie leaning on Pete's arm, guests and onlookers were awe-struck by the delight in Lizzie's face. Pete looked as if he could not quite believe his own good fortune. As they reached the door of the church, Lizzie laughed into the photographer's camera. Vicky followed her out of the church, Jimmy Scanlon by her side.

Gertie and Bill emerged, smiling and happy, knowing

that all the months of planning and preparation, and the strenuous journey, and the expense, had been worthwhile just to see the expression of pure joy on their youngest daughter's face. Karen leaned heavily on Paul's arm, conscious of her pregnancy.

The bells rang out as camera bulbs flashed. Peal after peal of joyous ringing filled the air, deadening the din of the traffic below. For a moment everyone was silent, and then laughter broke out with the relief of it all.

Pete led his bride to the waiting Cadillac.

Vicky settled Lizzie into the car, and arranged her dress around her, while the guests laughed and cheered.

The wedding breakfast was held in the dining-room of the Park Hotel. The long mahogany table had a table extended from either side of it, to accommodate everyone. Waiters wore white gloves, and served from silver salvers. Candles glowed on silver and crystal, and the garlands of roses that were on the altar were repeated at intervals on the table.

Pete and Lizzie sat at the head of the table.

'Happy, Mrs Scanlon?' Pete looked at Lizzie as if seeing her for the first time.

'Couldn't be happier.' Lizzie was flushed with the excitement of being the focus of attention, and kissed Pete several times between bursts of conversations with her parents, Vicky, Irene, Karen and Paul. Champagne corks popped, the guests stood up and glasses were raised to toast the happy couple.

'You look very pretty,' Auntie Peggy said to Karen.

'Thank you,' Karen said. 'Mustn't outshine the bride, though.'

'There's no fear of that. Sure isn't she the most beautiful sight on earth this minute?'

Auntie Peggy's eyes were on Karen's stomach as she leaned towards her. 'When's the baby due?'

'Early in August.'

'It's not long now. I hear you've been having a wonderful time with Paul's family.'

'Marvellous. And his dad was so thrilled to have him back. He's not well and wants Paul to take over the place.'

'What about Hank? Did you see him?' Aunt Peggy asked under her breath.

'He's in Germany at some forestry exhibition.'

'The right place for him. God keep him there. Are you going to stay on?'

'Eventually. John has to finish in the National School first, and I want to have my baby at home. Then we'll make plans.'

Karen was confident that the new baby would give Paul hope, and more incentive. She was also determined that he would participate in everything to do with her pregnancy, and the subsequent birth. She sipped her champagne and looked around at the guests. They were talking and laughing. Then Karen saw a woman come into the room.

She was dressed in a navy silk frock, with a knot of gardenias on one shoulder, and a matching cloche hat, the veil of which covered her eyes. High heels tapping on the maple floor, clutching a bag in her white-gloved hand, she made her way across the room. The men stopped chewing and stared, while the women sat in uneasy silence. By the time she reached the top table, their curiosity had almost got the better of them.

'Who is she?' John asked and was silenced with a quick 'Shhhh' from Karen. There was no recognition in Lizzie's face as she looked at her.

'Don't say you don't know me?' the voice drawled.

'I'm afraid not.' Lizzie's face had turned pink with embarrassment.

'Don't you make your old friends welcome at a showdown like this?' There was something familiar in the mocking voice.

'We certainly do.' Pete stood up, and leaning across the table, shook a white-gloved hand. 'You're welcome whoever you are.'

'You still don't know me?' The stranger lifted the veil back from her eyes. Lizzie shook her head.

'I'm May Tully.'

A gasp of disbelief reverberated around the table.

'May Tully!' Lizzie said as Gertie and Bill rose together to greet her. 'What are you doing in New York?'

'I'm auditioning for a part in *The King and I* on Broadway.' May smiled charmingly. 'When my mother wrote that you had all come over for the wedding, I thought how nice it would be to see you.'

'Good to see you too.' Vicky was beside her, eyeing her up and down, unable to hide her incredulity.

'Come and sit down. I heard you went to Hollywood to make a film,' Gertie said.

'So did I, but I didn't know you were a real film star,' Lizzie said. 'You look like one. Doesn't she, Pete?'

'She sure does.' Pete took a new handkerchief from his pocket and wiped mock perspiration from his brow.

Vicky called a waiter and ordered a meal for May, introducing her as 'a film-star friend from Hollywood'.

'What was the name of the film?' Jimmy Scanlon asked.

'*Road to Rio.*'

'Where you the star?'

'No. Dorothy Lamour was. I had a bit-part in it.'

'Oh, is that all?' Jimmy looked enviously at her.

'A great achievement.' Bill raised his glass and they all saluted May Tully.

Later Pete and Lizzie led the dancing, Pete grinning happily. Uncle Mike and Auntie Peggy stopped them on the floor to wish them every happiness.

'Well I'm happy anyway.' Pete gave his new wife a hug.

They danced on, stopping every minute to talk to people. The dancers swirled around, the colours of their dresses merging as they waltzed.

Auntie Sissy was dancing with John, Uncle Hermy with May Tully. Even Auntie Peggy, who hated any close bodily contact, let Uncle Mike twirl her around the floor, while Olive danced with Bill. The men drank pints, and the women – some of whom had never drunk before – sipped sweet sherry or wine.

Gertie relaxed with her glass of sherry, and was tapping her feet to the rhythm of the band. She paid no attention to John, who was playing hide-and-seek among the drapes with Jimmy Scanlon. When Olive complained that it was late, and that John was getting overexcited, Gertie said with a wave of her hand, 'Leave him alone. It's not every day my youngest daughter gets married.'

Gertie was exhausted, everything she had done since Lizzie's engagement – running her guest-house, cooking, cleaning, sewing, the long, tiring journey by ship, making sure everybody who came to the wedding was properly catered for – had drained her. Only now that the guests were obviously enjoying themselves was it safe to kick off her shoes. Time enough to recover when it was all over. Wouldn't she have the rest of her life to sit back with her memories to keep her company? It had been a successful wedding. Lizzie was a magnificent bride and Pete Scanlon was a handsome, well-liked groom.

When Pete slung the strap of his guitar over his shoulder, and began to strum it, Gertie could see how comfortable he was among family and friends, and how the girls who stood around to hear him sing looked admiringly at him. Who would have thought it, all those years ago when he was wounded in the war, that in this land of opportunity and prosperity he would make his mark and marry her daughter. If only his poor mother had lived to see it.

'My heart cries for you, sighs for you, dies for you,' he sang, as he gazed into Lizzie's eyes. Everybody cheered and began clapping their hands and tapping their feet to the rhythm. 'Come on Over to My Place' followed and 'Mocking Bird Hill' had everybody dancing, young with old, brother with sister. But it was 'Be My Love' that brought them to a standstill, and made them weep for love that was, or might have been, or could never be.

Gertie was remembering Pete and his dreams. He was ambitious too, she had to admit. Who could tell, they might come back to Ireland one day . . . She would hold on to her house for as long as she could, just in case. Meantime, Biddy would work there. Biddy was a hard-working, reliable girl, and Gertie knew that she liked working for her. She would help Biddy get on her feet.

'Excuse me, Mrs Doyle.'

Gertie looked up. The photographer was standing in front of her.

'Sorry to disturb you. If it's all right with you, I'd like to take one more group picture before the bride goes to change.'

'Certainly. I'll organize it.' Gertie rose and went to the microphone to make the announcement.

The group gathered in a semicircle with Pete and Lizzie in the middle.

'Say cheese,' the photographer called and his camera flashed several times.

Lizzie went to one of the rooms to change into her going-away outfit. Vicky accompanied her. Half an hour later they appeared at the top of the stairs. The group pressed forward. There was a cheer as they slowly came down the wide staircase, Lizzie dressed in a pale lilac matching coat and frock. A pill-box hat made of the same material sat neatly on her head, her curls brushed in around it. When they reached the bottom step, Lizzie tossed her bouquet in a wide arc. May Tully reached out and, tottering on her high heels, caught it.

'I'll invite y'all to the wedding when the time comes,' she drawled.

'But you're already married,' Jimmy Scanlon said.

'Shut your trap,' May scowled.

Vicky fussed over Lizzie, brushing her coat, and checking that her seams were straight. Someone began singing 'For they are jolly good fellows' and everyone joined in. The limousine purred outside while Lizzie lingered over the good-byes, with Pete calling to her to hurry up.

Bill held her tightly. 'Take care of my girl,' he said to Pete as he shook his hand.

Pete smiled. 'It'll be my pleasure.'

'Wrap up well. The nights are cold,' Gertie cautioned her daughter with one last hug.

'Don't worry. I'll keep her warm, Mrs Doyle.' Pete shook Gertie's hand and tightening his arm possessively around

Lizzie's waist drew her towards the swing doors. The couple crossed the foyer between the crush of guests waiting to wave them off. Two waiters held the doors open.

Lizzie and Pete went down the steps with their family and friends surging after them. Smiling happily, Lizzie blew kisses to everyone before stepping into the long black car. Pete climbed in beside her. As the car rolled away, there was a last glimpse of their faces through the rear window.

Vicky came to stand beside Gertie. 'Why am I crying?'

'I don't know. Why am I? We should be happy for them, and them off to Cape Cod.'

'We are.' They hugged one another.

'It'll be your turn next, Vicky.'

'Not for a long time.'

As the band struck up again, Vicky said, 'I'm going back to the dancing. Coming?'

They made their way to the ballroom where a handful of couples were slowly turning in the centre of the discarded tables.

Olive joined Gertie. 'Let's go and get ourselves a cup of coffee.'

She took Gertie's arm and escorted her to the lounge. It smelled of cigar smoke and faded perfumes.

'It was a good day,' Gertie sighed as she settled into an armchair.

'A wonderful day. Here's to the next big event.'

'Yes indeed.' Gertie was happy to think of the

forthcoming birth of Karen's baby, and marvelled at the wonders of life when there was something to look forward to.

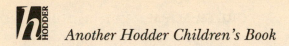

Another Hodder Children's Book

THE DAISY CHAIN trilogy

Part One

DAISY CHAIN WAR

By Joan O'Neill

Vicky asked to sit beside May Tully at school, with the excuse of getting help with her Irish. They walked home together ahead of me, sniggering at the boys. I hated them, and wished the war was over so that Vicky would go home. No such luck.

It is 1941, Britain is in the grip of the Second World War, and in Ireland, ten-year-old Lizzie Doyle is getting on with her life, trying to adjust to the 'Emergency' all around her, and the arrival of her wild cousin Vicky, from England. Vicky is trouble. She's a flirt, she's devious and she's headstrong. Can she and good-natured Lizzie ever be real friends?

'My favourite teenage book.' Robert Dunbar, *The Irish Times*

ORDER FORM

0 340 85466 9	DAISY CHAIN WAR	£5.99	❑
0 340 85467 7	BREAD AND SUGAR	£5.99	❑

All Hodder Children's books are available at your local bookshop, or can be ordered direct from the publisher. Just tick the titles you would like and complete the details below. Prices and availability are subject to change without prior notice.

Please enclose a cheque or postal order made payable to *Bookpoint Ltd*, and send to: Hodder Children's Books, 39 Milton Park, Abingdon, OXON OX14 4TD, UK.
Email Address: orders@bookpoint.co.uk

If you would prefer to pay by credit card, our call centre team would be delighted to take your order by telephone. Our direct line *01235 400414* (lines open 9.00 am–6.00 pm Monday to Saturday, 24 hour message answering service). Alternatively you can send a fax on *01235 500454*.

TITLE	FIRST NAME		SURNAME	
ADDRESS				
DAYTIME TEL:		POST CODE		

If you would prefer to pay by credit card, please complete:
Please debit my Visa/Access/Diner's Card/American Express (delete as applicable) card no:

Signature .... Expiry Date: ....

If you would NOT like to receive further information on our products please tick the box. ❑